TOXIC II: Antonio's Revenge

A Novel By
Lady Luck

Text QueenInk to 31996 for updates, early releases, and story of the month!

QueenInkPublishing.com

Contains explicit language & adult themes suitable for ages 16+

Be sure to LIKE our Queen Ink Publishing page on Facebook!

Introduction: Antonio

May 5th

Today is the big day, the day that I marry the love of my life. Marrying Jasmine is more than a dream come true; she has saved my life and introduced me to my higher self. Since being with her, I have learned what it means to be a real man; a man who is responsible, a provider, protector, compassionate, and a cultivator. She deserves to be a wife; she's already six months pregnant with our prince. There is something about today that I didn't experience when I married my first wife, Claire. It's real love, the love that makes you want to be a better man so she can be a better woman. Claire and I did not have a loving relationship. Instead, it was filled with greed, envy, covetousness, and sheer hatred. I am nervous as hell as I prepare to marry Jasmine, even more, I am grateful that her father has given me his blessing to do so. He's confident that I will protect her with everything in me for as long as I live. It was a mere coincidence that Jasmine and I even crossed paths; however, the fact that we fell in love and established a life together is a divine blessing from God.

Jasmine and I planned an intimate wedding on the white sands of Myrtle Beach, South Carolina. We agreed on a Royal Affair theme, accented with turquoise and white, which complement the transparent water. She has always dreamed of having a beach wedding, and I am honored to be her groom. Our bridal party is limited to four people, 50 guests, and a photographer. Jasmine wore all white and radiated angelic vibes, especially since she was carrying our son. Her bridesmaids are two of her childhood friends from North Carolina. They each wore different shades of blue: sky blue and baby blue. My groomsmen are childhood friends as well;

Tristan Banks has been my homeboy since grade school. My cousin, Kevin, is more like my brother as well. As a matter of fact, I haven't spoken with my blood brother, Tariq, in more than five years. That's another story for another day. Kevin and Tristan each wore an Egyptian blue colored tux, while I matched Jasmine's dress with white slacks and a white Pique Tuxedo. We were all barefoot and feeling free, which amplified the theme.

As Jasmine recited her vows, she began to cry, so I hugged her until she laughed. I whispered in her ear, "As long as there is breath in me, I will always speak life over you. You are my truest love and my other half." The pastor interrupts us with his pronouncement, we kiss, and finally, release the white doves. This is the most magical day that was ever created, and I'm grateful for it. We eat an elegantly styled dinner on the beach, complete with an open bar that offered champagne and top-shelf liquor. Her parents hired the finest caterers in South Carolina and an R&B band. It was definitely a party!

Now, back to my brother, Tariq. Tariq is incarcerated and we have a bit of a past that I don't discuss with anyone, not even my new wife. He called me this morning to complain about the attorney no longer working on his case. His lividness discouraged me from explaining to him the reason why the attorney was fired. "Listen, Tariq, your part of the money is gone, finito! Remember all the money you had me sending to your little girlfriends and homeboys? Well, that was also a part of your attorney fees, so I had to fire him once the money was depleted." "That's BULL SHIT Antonio, and we both know it. I know about your little business and how you have lines wrapped around the building, have celebrities partying there, and how you are making crazy dough every day. I thought we were family; I thought you were helping me fight the case. Or should I say *your case*." I know that my business is the talk of the town and his boys are telling him everything they hear and see. What they don't know is that this shit is a partnership between Jasmine and me, not my brother. He hangs up in my face when I tell him that I am not sending him a dime. Jasmine and I are stable, and she is totally oblivious to my past—and I intend to keep it that way. With her ex-boyfriend, Chris, finally out of the picture, we can begin our lives anew. My first-born son bears my namesake and is due to arrive three months from today. I am married to the most gorgeous woman alive, my business is a massive success, and I have built our dream home. What more could I ask for? Life is perfect just the way it is.

Four years later...

Chapter 1: Jasmine

Everything Happens for A Reason

The home was never this tranquil and serene during my teenage years; maybe my mental peace has transpired into my physical world. Finally, I can let my children experience the environment that nurtured me and the parents that raised me. Oh, what a journey! The vegetation of my parents' farm, my swing-set in the backyard, and my childhood room, which has walls plastered with Usher, Destiny's Child, and B2K bring forth a joyful nostalgia. The experience awed Jr. and our newest addition to the family, Jada, so much that they begged Antonio and me to let them stay with my parents this summer. If I do this would align perfectly because we were preparing to rebrand the business without the children interrupting every other minute. We have finally decided to open a new lounge and need to apply for commercial activity licenses, sign the necessary paperwork for leasing the building, and my favorite part, design the interior decor of the lounge. It was exhilarating to think of the new life that Antonio and I were creating for our family! New beginnings, a new mindset, and new love, aren't I blessed?

Antonio had never been to North Carolina, so he was just as intrigued as our children by the new territory. He decided to spend time with my dad by helping cut the wood for the fireplace. I love the bond that he is creating with my parents. The children are occupying themselves by playing in the leaf piles in the backyard. My daddy is finally realizing that I am no longer his baby girl but Antonio's wife. As for mommy, she is happy to have us all under one roof. I tell her about our goal to establish a lounge in North Carolina, and she supports us one hundred percent!

I left Antonio and the children at home while I attend a meeting for our new lounge. All that's left to do is sign off on the paperwork and discuss the details of revamping the place. I drove to the meeting blasting 90s jams the whole ride there. I walk into the building and take a deep breath before getting on the elevator. As I approach the front office, I hear the receptionist popping gum from the hallway. Please don't let this be a ghetto establishment! The receptionist looked like an extra from LL Cool J's "Around the way Girl" video; she sat at the front desk smacking on the gum so loudly that it echoed off the walls as a greeting. After standing at her desk for two minutes with no recognition, I cleared my throat and asked if anyone was available to help. She rolls her eyes to the back of her head before responding, "Oh my goodness, you've only been here a few seconds and you're already tripping. How may I help you?"

I really don't have the energy to entertain her shenanigans, so I ask her how long I will have to wait to meet with the manager. "I am here to meet with Mrs. Baker." She escorted me to Mrs. Baker's office. The decor was more than astonishing, it was majestic! It did not match the attitude of the receptionist but that can be addressed another day. Meanwhile, the tables, chairs, and walls were so elegant that I was afraid to sit down; it was quite lavish! Mrs. Baker's welcoming demeanor helped to ease my anxiety. The gigantic glass window offered a scenic view of the entire city. Mrs. Baker interrupts my daydream with a warm tone, "Hello, Mrs. Jennings, it's so nice to finally put a face with a name! I've heard nothing but great things about the lounge that was designed by both you and your husband. It is so refreshing to see a Black power-couple! We need a premier, nightlife lounge for elites and millennials. We would be delighted to have your business here in North Carolina!" I am elated by her kind remarks and exclaim, "Great!"

"We will schedule a viewing of the property next week. My receptionist will forward you the corresponding documents to begin the process!" I am still in a space of gratitude for all that Antonio and I have accomplished in such a short amount of time. First, the lounge in Atlanta, then the new properties, and now the new lounge in North Carolina—the sky's the limit!

But before I reach the sky, I have to go to the supermarket to buy snacks and food for dinner. As soon as I pull into the parking lot, I check my phone, only to find 20 missed calls from Antonio. When I call him back, I immediately squeal out of excitement, "Baby, we've got it! We got the space!" I hear my children in the background arguing about who will climb which tree the fastest. "Hey babe, that's great! I wish we could celebrate, but I'm judging the tree-climbing contest. How long before you come home? We're starving!" "I'm on my way to the supermarket now, so sit tight."

The more things change, the more they stay the same, especially in my little hometown. Every face is a familiar one, and they are all so fascinated that I live in Hotlanta. They are mostly wondering what happened between Chris and me. I don't have time for the gossip, so I grab my items and sprint out of the store. Before I can completely pull into the driveway Antonio is already running to the car to grab the groceries. Damn! What did I do to deserve this King? My mom and I bathe the babies, while the men chef up something in the kitchen. I really married a man who's just like my father! I head to the kitchen to see what's smelling so good and find Antonio pouring wine, lighting candles, and preparing the best table I've ever seen in my life. Tears of joy stream down my face. He notices my tears and rushes to wipe my face. "Jasmine, why the waterfalls? Our dreams are finally coming true, thanks to you. This is a celebration." I shared my concerns about opening a lounge in a new market, it is very intimidating. "I'm afraid of opening up the new lounge. What if people don't come. You know Atlanta is much different from Charlotte."

"You are the queen of interior decorating. This one will be just as grandeur as the first one." I leaned over to kiss him on the cheek and grab his little 'big' man. He smacks my ass and clenches my breast. "Damn, can we eat first, woman!" I stared into his eyes and kissed him as passionately as I did on our wedding day. We eat then race to the bedroom. I haven't put it on him like this since we made Jada. I am so grateful for this man.

My mom spoils us with home-cooked breakfast and fresh-squeezed orange juice! Daddy is sitting at the table reading the morning paper. He smiles when I walk in the kitchen. "Look who's finally up! Good morning, darling." I crack a smile. My phone interrupts our daddy-daughter moment. An unknown number appears on the screen, so I answer it with my professional voice.

"You finally know how to answer your damn phone." It's Chris. "What the hell is wrong with you, how did you get this number?" "Have you forgotten who I am? I saw you at the supermarket yesterday. We need to talk." "Saw me or stalked me?" "Jasmine, I don't have time for the bullshit. Come outside right now or I'll make a scene." I look out the window and see his car in the driveway. I tell my parents that I'm about meet with the manager of the property. He looks distressed, unhealthy, and unhappy; isn't the Chris that I once loved. The stench of alcohol and cigarettes reek from his clothes. His handicapped smile assured me that he had indeed let himself go after the tragedy.

"Are you out of your damn mind, Chris! I should have my husband kill you right now. What do you want?" He gazed into my eyes, and I felt the intense embarrassment that he had been wanting to relinquish since Antonio and I married. He bellows the most life-changing statement, "Look, your son is mine, not Antonio's." My ears are numb and my whole body becomes paralyzed with terror. I knew this day would come. I cannot confess that I have been questioning that myself.

"Boy, bye! Should I call my husband?" I can tell that he is not budging. We both know the truth. He hangs his head low. "Jasmine, I've been watching your family on Instagram, and day by day Jr. looks more like me. His posture, voice, and physical features come from me. I have pictures of me as a little boy that mirror Jr. When a man knows, he knows." My silence is deafening, and I played back the last time we had sex in my head to prove any doubt to his claims. "I won't leave until I get my son." "You shut the hell up! Shut up! He is NOT your son! Now get the hell out of my driveway!" He threatens to sue for custody. I stormed into the house and go straight to Antonio. "I need to talk to you, it's an emergency." I sigh heavily then spill everything. "Chris just came over here and is saying that Jr. is his son. If we don't get a paternity test, he's going to take it to the courts." His tone deepens. "What did you just say to me?" "I don't know if you are Jr.'s father." I murmured. He is infuriated. "I know damn well that just didn't come out your mouth?"

He had questions, but I had no answers. Ashamed, I tried to explain to him that Chris was my first, and I've never been pregnant. "When I met you, I was at a bad place in my life, I was so vulnerable and confused. I naturally assumed that you were the father." I kneel in front of him and massage the tension from his hands. He looks defeated, I feel like I've committed the worst crime known to mankind. "Damn, Jasmine! I told you to stop fucking with this man, but you just had to stay to "work it out"! Now, look at this shit." Tears were welling in his eyes. "You mean to tell me that Jr. is not my son? Are you serious?" Seeing him cry shatters my entire world. I can't take it any longer, so I go to my Mom's room. I collapse in her arms.

"How could this happen?" I told her everything, not leaving out one detail. "Well, honey, Chris was taking you through a lot, it's not purely your fault. Antonio knew your situation when you met him. I'm sure it's a misunderstanding. In the meantime, I'll keep my grands here for the summer so that you and Antonio can work things out." She knew what to say to ease my spirit now I don't have to beg her to let them stay after all. I normally wouldn't agree to such an extended stay, but she reassured me that her sister was bringing our little cousins from New York. "I'll have all the backup I need, trust me, everyone will be on toddler duty!" I hug her then go upstairs to tell Antonio the plan. He has our bags already packed and is giving me the silent treatment. It is going to be a long ride home.

Chapter 2: Tariq

Manslaughter

I have been pinned up in the US Penitentiary, Atlanta for a decade with no ounce of freedom in sight. Being around all of these men has finally taken its toll on me, and I am ready to bounce! I may do some dumb shit so that the guards will throw me in solitary confinement. Man, you know it is a sad case when a man is plotting his way to the hole. I am so over this shit! But I'm going to keep my cool and play it safe. Prison is not permanent, and I will never get accustomed to this lifestyle. I have never been so dehumanized in my life, especially for a crime that I didn't commit by myself. My brother is dead to me from here on out, and I will never enlist myself in this hellhole again. Never again!

This penitentiary should be demolished onsite; the food is atrocious and barely edible. The rooms are surrounded by mildew, and the library is only open one day a week. A man can't even escape his sorrows through education because the system wants to make sure you are miserable. The rooms don't have windows, and we are only allowed to go outside once a month, so tell me the difference between this and solitary confinement? At least while I'm in the hole, I don't have to hear these grown-ass men complain about how innocent they are or how the system set them up for failure since birth. When are these men going to learn how to take some accountability for their actions? We all know the school-to-prison pipeline is some institutionalized racism bullshit but please, take accountability for your actions. See, that's why I can't bang with my pussy ass brother, Antonio. This man was cool with me taking the fall by myself, and like a dumbass, I complied. Talk about brotherly love, this man has stopped putting money on my books, fired my attorney and is living the good life in the A. Big ass house, lounges, wife, kids; I wouldn't be surprised if he had some side-chicks in a condo in Buckhead. That's how grimy and sneaky this man is. But enough about him, I'm happy I have my brothers from the hood who have been holding me down from day one. If no one else has my back, I know my homies will always look out for me.

"Mr. Jennings, your attorney would like to meet with you." My Corrections Officer has a thing for the kid, so I hope she's not trying to role-play right now because I am not in the mood. I let her give me head, and after that, she's been on me like hair on soap. "Listen, baby, not today, I have too much going on right now. I'm trying to get my mind right.
"She walks over to me, licks her thick, succulent lips, and whispers in my ear,
"Oh, this is not a game, there's a cutie in the lobby who claims to be able to get you off. Question is, when can you get me off?" She swirls her tongue around my ear and then bites it so hard that I can't help but crack a smile. "Come on with the shenanigans; take me to see this fairy-attorney."

She escorts me to the lobby and then winks her eye. "Let me know if I can be of any assistance. "The attorney looks like he is barely out of college, let alone Law School. But hell, at this point, I'll take anybody. He has a North Carolina pendant on, so he might be from Queen City.

"Hello, Mr. Jennings, my name is Christopher Davis, and I would like to present to you a once in the lifetime get out of jail free card. I know you are not completely guilty and did not commit that robbery alone. If you let me help you, you won't regret it. I will represent you for free."

"What do you want in return? This sounds too good to be true. And how the hell did you find me?"

"Let's say I did my research. I have scrutinized your files and learned that you have an extensive criminal background in burglary, murder, drug trafficking, illegal possession of firearms, and multiple violations of probation. You even managed to destroy your house-arrest monitoring device. I have obtained footage from your last bank robbery and let's say the accomplice isn't one of my favorite people."

First, how does the negro know so much about my life?
"Well, I have already confessed to killing the security officer."

"But there is no tangible supporting evidence of such a murder. Plus, I saw who really shot the officer. All you have to do is work for me."

"Man, hell no. You're going to have to find another way to get me off because I'm done talking about this shit here."

"I understand that you don't want to snitch. However, I do have an important question; is Antonio Jennings your brother?"

This is too coincidental; how does he know that Antonio is my brother? I am tired of being locked up in this place. Furthermore, it's not fair that Antonio is walking around with wads of cash that he did not earn by himself. Shit, I may as well take ole boy up on his offer. What do I really have to lose? Do I really want to rot in this place? I decided to give in.

"You know what? I'm down. Let's teach this man a well-deserved lesson."

He is giddy as hell about my giving in. "Great, Mr. Jennings! It will be my pleasure to get you out of here as soon as possible."

"Sounds good, so when can do I get out of here? You don't worry about anything I'll handle everything.

"I only one condition, take Antonio down for everything that he has. If you can do that for me, then consider your fees waived."

"Say no more. I have been waiting for ten years to avenge that snake. But one thing, how do you know Antonio and me?"

"Let's just say I know a little bit of everything. Do we have a deal?"

"You damn right we do. I'm ready to start right now."

We shook hands to seal the deal. Chris only had one order, "Whatever you do, don't lay a finger on his wife and children."

The guard escorted me to my cell, and I begged him to let me make one phone call.

"15 seconds only."

I call my girl and let her know that I am on my way home, so she needs to arrange for my arrival. "Are you serious, babe? How? When?"

"I can't talk now; just get ready I'll call you."

The guard unplugs the cord to the phone right in the middle of my conversation. Chris is an angel sent from heaven! I finally get to my cell and don't utter a word about my freedom. A week later the same guard comes back to escort me to the administrators so that I can process my papers. This is a dream come true. "All right, Mr. Jennings, you are free to go. I don't want to see you back, so, stay out of trouble!"

My bottom chick, Tasha, is waiting for me in the parking lot, and I must say, she looks just as good today as she did ten years ago. She's not marriage material because she loves to rip the streets. Nonetheless, I am excited to see her. I walk up to her and smack her on the ass; she grabs my dick so hard I almost fall to my knees. We both start laughing, and she passes me the keys to the whip. The route home is the same, but the scenery is much different. I feel like I'm in a new world. See, that's what prison does to you, it quarantines you from reality. The McDonald's that was on the Boulevard is now a big ass condominium, the Blockbuster that was on the corner of the exit is now an Apple store, and the casino that used to steal all my money is now a church. Not to mention her car has fancy-ass rear-view interior camera features on the dashboard. And how the hell are phone calls able to come through the car?

"Damn, baby, you sure weren't missing any meals, were you?" We both crack up laughing.

"All I had time to do was lift weights and exercise. I know you don't like no skinny nigga."

She pulls a stash of weed from her bra and rolls a fat ass blunt for us to puff. "Welcome home, Daddy. "I take two puffs and almost had a heart attack. That's the good shit, I can already tell. Smoke surrounded the car so badly that I had to pull over at the nearest exit. Before I could even switch gears, my girl leaned over to unzip my pants. She pulled my dick out and started sucking like she was in a tootsie roll licking contest. Shit was sloppy, juicy, hot, and wet as fuck. Damn, this shit is heaven on earth. She peeps up to glance at my eyes then proceeds to blow on my dick and caress my jewels. This shit feels so good I can't help but bust a nut in her mouth. She takes a big gulp of my nut and smacks her lips like it was the best beverage to quench her thirst. I love how confident she is while she's doing her thing, shit turns me on!

We finally pull up to my old hood, and I see my homie posted on the porch. He looks as though he's just seen a ghost, "Damn, man, how the hell you get out so early? You must be snitching behind those walls?"

"Na, I have connections! I got this lawyer kid representing me, and he was able to get me out mad early. All he needed was a little favor from ya boy."

He looks puzzled. "A favor, from you? I don't know if I trust that."

"One word: Antonio."

"Your brother, Antonio? The same Antonio who let you take the rap for that bullshit robbery you all left me out of?"

"Damn right. My brother and the attorney have beef over some chick. Antonio supposedly went off and married the girl, so Chris wants me to set him up. The crazy shit is, this man knows me like the back of his hand. He mentioned things that Antonio and I did when we first got in the game 20 years ago. I was a little hesitant at first, but since I haven't spoken with my brother in a decade, fuck him. I can't believe he stopped coming to visit me." He shakes his head, "This is some wild shit, boy!"

"Tell me about it. Antonio stopped sending me money and then all of a sudden, I didn't have a lawyer anymore. I never told the cops about his part in the burglary. The plan was for him to get me out in five years. It's not fair that he got to get off scot-free."

My homeboy is a truck driver and delivers arms all across the country, so it shouldn't be hard to get my hands on a tool. He was the reason we were able to rob banks without a trace until Anthony pulled the trigger on the security guard and shot his ass dead. I can tell that my homie is thinking of a master plan.

"Man, we need to do a hit soon. I need some real cash. Shit hasn't been right since you haven't been home. You down?"

He put his hand out for me to shake on the deal. I accepted with no hesitation.

"Like two flats on a Cadillac."

Chapter 3: Antonio

Time Heals All Wounds

Words can't express how happy I am to have a break from the kids. Since Jas and I never got a chance to have a real honeymoon, maybe we can use this summer to please each other and blow off some steam. Enough about the lovey-dovey stuff, I am happy to see that Jasmine is feeling better and focusing on marketing the new lounge. I know it's a struggle to manage the staff at the Atlanta lounge as well as ensure that the decor is competitive and upscale. Maintaining two businesses is not as bad of an idea as I thought! The best thing about it is that we can afford all that expensive shit in Ikea, Macy's, Pier 1 Imports, and her favs, Bed Bath and Beyond. Those stores have always been her happy places to escape to whenever she was going through a hard time, so it's no surprise that she is retreating to them even more frequently now. I have never heard someone speak so passionately about completing an inventory list, upgrading a Pinterest board, and sketching out a mock blueprint for the Charlotte location. No matter what happens, Jas keeps me smiling. I'm not letting Chris punk-ass mess this up either. He doesn't even know that I can end his whole life with one phone call, and no one would suspect a damn thing. All I know is that he better leave my wife the hell alone before I help him meet his maker.

I take a second to pause and reflect on how grateful I am for the life that I have. It's more than I could have ever imagined. A ride or die woman who is quadrupling our income, two beautiful kids, and my mother-in-law's cancer is in remission. What more could a man ask for? Jas sends me some swatches for the new color, we agree on dark turquoise and silver. The bar will be an ombre gradient of various shades of turquoise and silver; the bar stools will be upholstered to match the walls. Completing maintenance on the new location is stress-relieving. I almost lost it after she told me that bullshit Chris approached her with, but I am slowly regaining my sanity after going through a deep depression. I need to forgive her because it's not her fault. I know that Jr. belongs to me and I refuse to let Chris mind-fuck us.

On some real shit though, it has been like walking on eggshells in the house, especially when I mention the kids. I guess she's upset with me for insinuating that all of this is her fault. When those words hit my lips, I knew I would end up swimming with the sharks. Deep down I know that it isn't her fault, but I was so mad that I blurted it out. Since she endured so much at the hands of my ex-wife and her relationship with Chris, she is still on prescribed anxiety medication to this day. I need to man up and be there for her, even if it hurts me. This shit is no joke, and I swear I could have this man bodied with one word. But that lifestyle is behind me, and Jasmine doesn't know that side of me. I damn sure don't need her learning about my past life. It was a gruesome part of my life. These days I am a changed man, I don't associate with those cats I kicked it with when I was thuggin'. I maintain my composure around Jas, no matter the cost.

On my way home I stopped by the florist to order a custom bouquet. I order the white roses and have the designer accent a 'J & A' with red roses in the middle. Then, I head to the liquor store to grab a bottle of Merlot for her and Bourbon for myself. I creep in from the back door and find Jasmine washing dishes with Mary J. Blige in the background. I already know what time it is; she's getting upset, and I calm her down, by sneaking up on her with the flowers behind my back, she glances at them and rolls her eyes. "Don't speak to me, Antonio! I know that you think it's my fault, so don't try to woo me now." Mary J. Blige's, *I'm Not Gon' Cry* plays next, and Jasmine scrubs a plate so hard that it breaks. Her pain is so potent that it pierces my soul. I hug her tightly. She cries in my chest, clenching my back for dear life. I whisper in her ear, "Baby, I'm sorry for the way I've been acting lately. The thought of my son not being mine scared the shit out of me. I apologize for resenting you. I love y'all more than life itself and would do ANYTHING to protect my family." She inhales and exhales loudly.

"I know baby, but when you said it was my fault, I lost it. Throwing the blame on me is not fair."

I smother her and lift her up to wrap her legs around me. We kiss passionately, and I can feel her body loosening. She's wearing the pink lace boy shorts that I bought her for Valentine's Day a few years ago, the same ones she wore when we made Jada. I slide them down her legs with my teeth and bend down to taste her delicate meadows. She moans softly, as I swish my tongue around her pussy lips. I can't tell which is wetter, my mouth or her lips! She quivers and shakes uncontrollably, all while gripping my neck. I continue to brush my tongue up against her little, pink flower, swallowing all her juices with delight. She likes it when I blow on her pussy, so I send a gust of wind to send her to the top. She screams loudly and arches her back. I take a break and use this as my opportunity to ask for forgiveness, "Do you forgive me?" She blurts out, "YES!" before squirting all over my face. This is the best facial I've ever had!

She whispers, "Let me suck your dick." I kiss her pussy one last time before standing up and whipping out my little, big man. She swirls her tongue around the head and clenches my ass. My dick swells up hard as shit, so she yanks it out of her mouth and motions for me to put it in. She rides it as if it's the first time we've fucked. She performs a Kegel exercise on my dick, increasing the urgency for me to cum inside of her. "You know you want to, daddy. Cum inside your pussy, you've never had it like this before. Your wifey has been practicing!" I grant her request and alleviate the stress, tension, and anxiety that I have been holding in for weeks.

As soon as I prepare to devour her pussy again, I am interrupted by the doorbell.

"Keep going," she moans. "They'll go away. I need this." I finish my job, only to hear the doorbell ring back to back. I become extremely irritated and finally yell, "Hold the fuck up!" We both scramble to get dressed, and I send Jasmine upstairs to load my gat. I grab the second one in case our visitor gets carried away. I've been taking her to the gun range so she can protect herself whenever I am not around. I know she's fired up and ready to go!

"Who is it?" I bark. I peep through the hole, and a cloud of smoke blinds my view of the person. "Open the damn door little ass Ant, before I sting yo' ass!"

Tariq is the only one who says that lame shit. He's been saying it since we were kids! How the fuck did my brother get to my house? More importantly, how did he get out of jail so soon? He had at least five more years in the joint. I open the door and cock my gun behind my back in case he tries some sneaky shit. The last time I saw him was when he popped that security guard at our last bank robbery. He took all the charges for that case. Seeing Tariq was like seeing a ghost from the past. He has a fresh pair of Jordan's on, along with a New Era fitted, so I can tell this was not his first stop. All I know is that he better not starts any shit. He takes another puff of his splif and blows the smoke in my face. He sarcastically asks, "Happy to see me?" "What the hell are you doing here?" I ask. "Damn, that's not the welcome home I was expecting, but hey, at least you answered the door. Damn, you're living large!" I text Jasmine:

Me: "Stay upstairs. I'll explain everything later."

He brushes past me and barges into the house. "How did you get home so quickly?"

"I was released on good behavior." He has a smirk on his face that says otherwise. "Where's the wife, two kids, and a picket fence?" I know my brother is up to something, this is too suspicious. "How did you find out where I lived?" He walks further into the house, looking like he's ready to set up shop.

"Let's just say a little birdie told me. It's not a problem, is it? I mean, I am your blood brother. Don't do me greasy now that you're out here living the American Dream."

Jasmine comes downstairs and looks stoic, "Antonio, who's this?" I am embarrassed to say, especially since I have never told her that I have a brother. But I opt to tell the truth because I can't lie to her.

"Jasmine, this is my brother. Please, go upstairs." My tone is stern, so she goes upstairs without question.

The tension is so thick you can cut it with a machete.

"Did I come at the wrong time? A little trouble in paradise? You mean to tell me your little lady doesn't know that you are a gangster?"

"FUCK YOU, Tariq!" I yell. He laughs.

"I see you're living the good life; married to a beautiful woman, have two beautiful babies. Perfect family, huh, Ant?" He says as he holds my family picture.

"Word on the block is that you've got the hottest lounge in Atlanta right now, too." He throws my family picture against the wall so hard that the glass frame shatters.

"FUCK ME? NO, FUCK YOU! YOU'D RATHER I BE

FUCKED UP IN THAT CELL WHILE YOU'RE OUT LIVING LAVISH. YOU'RE LIVING OFF OF SOME SHIT THAT WE WORKED HARD FOR. YOU OWE ME BIG TIME, AND I THINK THAT'S THE PART YOU'VE FORGOTTEN ABOUT. SO, FUCK YOU!"

His eyes are bloodshot red. I stand there trying not to blow his brains out.

I remind him, "I don't owe you a damn thing! I sent you half of your money! I sent the rest to your little girlfriend, as you requested. I kept my portion and invest it. That's the end of it; I don't owe you a damn thing. As I see it, we're even."

"But I'm not the one who killed the security guard! He side-eye me. You right but if I hadn't killed him your punk ass would have been dead! Antonio, I saved your life by taking the charge, and this is how you repay me? Damn, guess I'm Gee-Money, and you're Nino Brown because you sure as hell are not my keeper!"

"Keep your damn voice down! I don't give a fuck what you say, that shit has nothing to do with me."

"Ant, we both agreed that no matter what happens if one of us goes down the other lookout, no matter what happens. You violated the code. Does your girl even know who you are?"

I am ashamed at the fact that Jasmine knows little to nothing about my past, let alone that I robbed banks for a living not selling drugs as my ex-wife Claire had thought. Hell, half of that bank money was used to renovate our properties, but it was washed clean by then, I can't let her know all this shit.

"Don't worry about what my wife knows. If I find out that you've had any contact with her or my children, your ass will pay. This time it'll be a permanent cell!"

"Chill big dawg; I want to get to know my family. Shouldn't Jr. and Jada know their uncle?"

I don't know who is giving him inside information on my family, but as soon as I find out, all hell will break loose. Hell, maybe I am the evil one. Tariq could sense my anxiety, so he used it as an opportunity to make a proposition.

"You know what, your secret is safe with me, under one condition. Let me live here for a few weeks until I get my shit together. Plus, I want part ownership of the lounge."

At this point, I couldn't care less about his proposition. I'm going to give in until I get to the bottom of this shit. Who sent him? Who's giving him information about my wife, children, my life? I let it slide because a part of me does feel guilty, especially since he did all of the time for a crime that both of us committed.

Chapter 4: Jasmine

Should Have Known Better

I know that I am depressed if I'm washing dishes willingly. I usually load the dishwasher with the quickness and go on about my day, but today is different. Today, I need to calm my nerves and gather my thoughts. Oddly enough, washing the dishes is giving me the tranquility that I desire. Maybe the water is washing away the pain. For the first time, I feel uncomfortable in my own house. It is no longer a home that Antonio and I created, suddenly, it has become a halfway house. Tariq living here has been a major adjustment; he's becoming a distraction to our lives. I would be lying if I said that I did not feel vulnerable when I am alone in the house with him. My emotions are all over the place, and I don't know how to feel around Antonio, his brother, or even myself. I have yet to tell Antonio about the nightmares that I have been having about Claire and Dre's kidnapping. I admit, I am traumatized and probably should seek professional help. I am at a crossroads right now and don't know which way to turn. Maybe Antonio and I should seek marital counseling so that we can get everything out on the table. Chris has constantly been blowing my phone up ever since he brought up this DNA test nonsense. He is complaining about Antonio refusing to take the test, claiming he already knows the truth. I pull some tricks out my hat and finally get him to agree to it. What if Jr. is Chris' son? What if my husband doesn't trust me anymore? What if I keep having these damn nightmares about Claire? What if—

"Shit! If I break another glass plate, I am going to lose it!" I kneel on the floor, carefully pick up the minced glass, and sob loudly, forgetting that I am not in the house alone.

"Good morning, beautiful. Is everything ok?" Tariq interrupts my pity party with his sultry voice. I am so vexed with my thoughts that I can feel the tears welling in my eyes. I can't let him see me cry because I know he'll attempt to console me. Even worse, I know I will oblige. He resembles Antonio so much that I can't focus on sweeping the glass. Am I mentally cheating on Antonio with his jailbird brother? He seems like a compassionate man who is trying to find his way. I look up at him from the floor, only to see him wrapped in a towel from the waist down. He just got out of the shower, and I can still see the misty steam lingering from his body. His skin is glistening, damn this man is fine as hell! His body is a piece of art; his very presence commands attention and demands respect. Tariq's lips are full and succulent, and his legs look as though he just placed first in a 5k marathon. His skin is a smooth, hazelnut complexion with red undertones. Ty and Ant look identical just a shade difference. To top it all off, Ty has the nerve to be bearded. I know that Tariq is a felon, but my husband is no angel himself. I can't believe he kept his former lifestyle from me; I thought we were in this together. I immediately evaporate those thoughts from my mind and focus on the task at hand: getting the hell away from Tariq.

"I need a moment to be alone. I'll be ok. Would you mind cleaning this up for me? I need to get ready to handle some business." He stares at me, extends his arm to pick me up, and slowly lifts me to my feet. I am sure not to make eye contact with him.

"Tell me, again, how did you and my brother meet?" That is a touchy subject, and I sure as hell don't want to go down memory lane, so I omit some details from the story.

"Well, before Antonio, I was madly in love with my high school sweetheart, Chris. He's some big shot lawyer now. Anyway, he attended law school with Antonio's ex-wife, Claire. Not sure if you met her or not, but she cheated on Antonio with Chris and made all of our lives a living hell with her fatal antics. Your brother and I met unexpectedly and did not know that we had mutual acquaintances. Long story short, I ditched Chris' cheating ass and got with Antonio. It has been one of the best decisions of my life."

He looks stunned. "Wow, y'all have been through the fire. Well, Miss. Lady, go ahead and handle your business. I'll be here when you get back. If you need anything, remember, I am here for you…as a brother."

I nod my head, smile, and run to my room. If I am left five more seconds alone with Tariq, I'm sure I will be a dead woman. Antonio is the love of my life, and I wouldn't trade our marriage for anything in the world. Antonio is texting me now.

Antonio: "Hey, baby, have you seen my ID? I can't find it anywhere. I just got pulled over, and thankfully the cop let me go. When you get a chance can you look for it? Thanks, baby girl."

Why is my husband always losing something? As soon as I get ready to respond to Antonio my Mom video chats me. She looks distressed; her eyes are puffy, and I can tell she has been crying.

"Is everything ok, Mom? Are my kids driving you crazy? You know you can spank their butts!" She hesitated before she spoke.

"Jasmine, Christopher just came over with a DNA test for Jr. I couldn't stop him because he had a warrant and a police officer. I got a glimpse of the paper, and it read "DNA Diagnostic Center." Honey, Jr.'s confused, Jada was screaming, I'm a frantic mess, ——thank goodness your father hasn't come home yet. He would have been livid, and someone would have gone to jail. I don't know what you have going on, but this has to be fixed as soon as possible!"

"Wait, what! Are you serious? Is my baby ok?"

"He's fine; I told him that his parents would explain everything to him. He's sitting at the table eating now."

"He is overstepping his damn boundaries! I apologize for my mouth, Mom, but this man is trying to ruin my life."

"Well, you are your father's child." She scolds me and presses her lips tightly. "This is getting too messy. Fix this Jasmine."

She hangs up the phone in my face. I take a deep breath and prepare to call Chris. I call four times in a row, but he sends each one to voicemail. This M'effer has lost his mind! I throw my phone on the floor out of frustration.

Tariq yells from the kitchen, "Everything ok?" "I'm fine!"

I grab my car keys and head over to the lounge. I listen to gospel music to keep from crying. I arrive at the lounge and find my husband behind the bar mixing drinks for a few customers. His face illuminates when he sees me. Therefore, why I married this man.

"Speaking of my backbone, here she is now. Baby, what are you doing here so early? You found my ID?" I don't want to make a scene in front of our customers, so I storm to the back of the club, and he follows me.

"Chris has fucked up big time! He went to my parent's house and swabbed a DNA test on Jr.!" Antonio is infuriated and looks at me the same way he did when I told him Chris pushed me down a flight of stairs a few years ago.

"I'm going to handle this the way I should have years ago. I should have killed his ass when I had the chance, but I wanted the brother to live. But this is the last straw. He is a dead man walking." I can tell that he is not calling a bluff.

"Don't say that, baby. I don't want you in jail. Let's think about this."

"Jasmine, I will never do anything to put our family at risk, I will never leave you. But that man has disrespected us for the last time." He walks away to make a phone call; I assume he's calling somebody from his past. Chris finally calls back.

"Yeah, did you call?"

"You know damn well I called, don't play games with me because I'm not in the mood for this! What you did was foul and against our agreement. My husband agreed to take your little test, and then you bring drama to my parent's house. This shit is not a game, Chris." He chuckles.

"Why are you scared of me getting this DNA test? If you're so sure that he belongs to your gangster husband, you should have nothing to worry about. You know just like I know that Jr. is my son."

"I'm not worried about me; I'm scared for you."
"For Me?" He asks, "Why?"

"You became a person I don't know anymore. You are making these rash decisions that can lead you down a path of no return. Don't forget what happened to your ex-girlfriend, Claire."

His voice begins to shake, and for the first time, I feel sorry for him.

"Jasmine, this was supposed to be my family, our family. But you chose Ant—"

"Chris, Stop! No, no, no! You are not about to flip this on me! You chose Claire and work. You made decisions just like I did. So do not blame this on me."

"Well, since I can't have my family, I am going to fight for my son. I'm sending those papers to the lab today, and once they prove that I am Jr.'s father, I am suing you for custody. It's not a damn thing you or Antonio can do to stop me. By the way, how are you enjoying your new houseguest?" I hang up in his face— that son of Bitch!

Chapter 5: Tariq

Robbing Identities

When will I ever give this hustling shit up? Man, I'm glad that Chris was able to get me out of the pen, but now I feel like I'm his little pawn. It appears his life's mission is to plot against my brother, and here I am, selling my soul to help him do it. Ant and I may not see eye to eye on everything, but at the end of the day, that's blood, and it doesn't get any thicker. This is the last dummy mission that I'm going to do for Chris. Whatever he wants to do to sabotage my brother, he gone need to do it alone. My conscious is getting the best of me, let me smoke a blunt and get this shit over with. Matter of fact, I'm giving up the entire street life, I don't even get excited off this shit no more.

So much shit is going through my mind while I wait for Chris to come to scoop me. First, why the fuck didn't I run into Jasmine's fine ass first? I bet her pussy is bomb as hell, especially if she has two greedy men fighting over her. I had a dream about her a few nights ago, I was fucking her brains out, then my brother walked in, and he shot my ass. Seriously though, I've caught her staring at my notch a few times, so I wish she would lie and say she hasn't thought about fucking me.

Chris finally pulls up, and as usual, he looks drunk as hell. Man, this shit must have taken a toll on him. He limps his way to the car, flask in one hand and car keys in the other. He looks at me as if I'm a hero of some sort.

"My main man, Tariq! Are you ready to get this bag of money? I know this is light work for you, so you should be in and out in under 4 minutes, right?" For the first time since my first robbery, I feel guilty before committing the crime. I take a long puff and flick the butt of my blunt out of the window.

"The rental is parked adjacent to the bank. It is black and unmarked; I'll stay right here and wait."

"We're wasting a lot of time; let's get this shit over and done with." I pull my black skull mask with the net eye-holes over my face, put on my gloves to conceal my fingerprints, and dash out of the car. My Beretta is tucked on the left interior pocket of my coat just in case someone doesn't want to cooperate. I make sure to open the door at exactly 9:30 am because that is when the guards are least expecting it. I stand in the shortest line and tell the teller to give me all the money out of the safe and to remove the dye pack if she wants to keep her life. I pass her the duffle bag to deposit the money and instruct her to stay calm, or I will blow her brains out all over this counter.

"Hurry up! You're taking too long!" Her co-worker follows her.

"Where the fuck is you going? Stay your ass here where I can see you or I'm firing!" While she's doing that, I drop Antonio's ID on the floor and order everyone to lie on the ground until the transaction is completed. As soon as the teller passes the bag to me, I see her nod her head to the guard, so I react by turning around and firing a bullet in the direction of the guard. He chokes and falls to his knees, blood rapidly spewing from his mouth. I hear people whimpering; then a deafening siren sounds off to alert the police of the robbery. I rush to the rental car and jump in the back seat of Chris's unmarked car.

"Fuck! Fuck! Fuck! That wasn't supposed to happen! I fucked up! Shit did not go according to plan; the motherfuckers put a new guard on the floor! Man, I scoped this place out for two weeks, and this is the first time that I'm seeing this new guard. I saw him die right before my eyes!"

"Calm down! He knew what time it was when he applied for the job. Give me the bag and let's get the fuck out of here."

"All your selfish ass cares about is framing my brother. Take me the fuck home!"

"You don't call the shots around here, Ty! Let's remember who got who out of jail. Let's remember our deal, or I'll ship your ass back to the big house with one phone call. You do what I say, not the other way around. We're making a detour to my crib." We arrive at his house, which is more like a shack, and I understand why he is so eager to break up my brother's family: emptiness. The walls are a dingy white, the carpet is mildew, and there is no love or life in the air.

"Have a drink with me, Ty. I need to clear my mind for a minute." He pours me a shot of Jack Daniels and mixes Hennessy and Coca-Cola for himself.

He turns on the TV, only to see breaking news of the bank that I just robbed. The teller who gave me the money was uncontrollably shaking as she tries to describe my appearance. My stomach turned and all of a sudden I felt nauseous. Damn, who knew I had a conscious? The news reported that the guard I shot was in critical condition but was expected to live. Thank GOD!

"So, what are you going to do with that money?" I ask Chris.

"Don't worry about it. My son and I are going to skip town after the test proves what I already know. This money is what I need to give my son the proper life he deserves. I'm telling you now; your brother will never see my son again for the rest of his living days. Jas can take a lot of things away, but she can't take my son. I can't wait until I show them the results!"

I bark back "She looks so happy, you know? Why would you want to ruin that?"

"That was supposed to be my family. I ruined it, and now I'm going to fix it."

He assured me that he would take care of everything from here and that I don't have to worry about doing any more jail time. He turns off the TV, and we head out of the door.

"Wait, you did remember to drop Antonio's ID at the bank, right?"

"Yessuh, Boss, I did everything you told me to."

"Save the sarcasm, please. Let's go."

Chris caught me staring at him with a puzzled face. "What? What's the problem?"

"You must have some big nuts; people don't usually fuck over my brother and get away with it. I'm surprised he didn't kill your ass a long time ago." He brushed me off and said, "I'm not worried about Antonio." "Alright, man, do what you do. Take me home and lose my number. I have no reason to know you anymore. You got your DNA test, you got your money, and you got me out of jail. That was the deal. As a matter of fact, I'm going to find my own way home. Get yourself together."

Chapter 6: Antonio

Here We Go Again

Just when everything seems to be going well, something fucked up has to happen. I'm finally getting adjusted to Tariq, Jas and I have officially made up, and we have at least another four weeks before the kids come home. Life couldn't be any better. I can't believe this sorry excuse for a man thinks that my son is his. I'm definitely not having it. But for now, I only concern myself with our new business. I am so excited for the second location in Charlotte because I know that it will bring a new level of success to our family. Queen City, your queen is ready for her crown! It feels so good to hold Jas in my arms again and protect her; I would kill over, her and she knows it. I get her in the mood by giving her a foot massage; I can tell that she has some tension by the way she squirms when I press certain points.

"Damn Ant, you trying to put another baby in me? Hell, forget opening another lounge; we need to establish a massage business!"

"Somebody has jokes! But on the real, I don't care what happens, as long as our family is together, our daughter, and *our son*."

My phone disrupts our intimate moment, and it's my General Manager.

"Hey, Mr. Jennings, I'm sorry to bother you so late, but someone had an allergic reaction to the seafood sampler. Your assistant manager failed to tell them that crabs and shrimp were in the sampler and he is allergic to shellfish. There wasn't a disclosure about the dish on the menu either, so we have to take the blame. I hate to say this, but we may have a lawsuit awaiting us."

"Damn, if it's not one thing, it's another. I'm on my way so don't answer any questions, inform others that you can't speak on the matter without an attorney present. Close the restaurant early."

As I drive to the lounge, I contemplate on how long it took Jasmine and me to build the lounge to an upper-echelon status and how easily it could all be taken away due to a careless mistake. Although the menu disclosure was the responsibility of the General Manager, I have to take full responsibility for everyone else's fuck up. In hindsight, this may be a life lesson that I need to stay on my toes at all times, whether I am at work, home, or in the streets. I hope we're able to settle out of court because I cannot afford to take another L this year.

When I arrive at the lounge, my attorney, Tristan Banks, is already there speaking to the manager, so I am not too worried. Tristan and I have been working together for at least ten years, basically since he began his career. If it weren't for Tristan, my ass would have been sentenced to life in prison. He is a general attorney that knows the law like the back of his hand. Criminal Law, Business Law, and Entertainment Law are his areas of expertise. Tristan has assured us that this will not have a chance to make the headlines since the person was aware that most samplers include most types of seafood. To that degree, there was some negligence on the customer's part. The customer must have been so afraid that he called the police because two police cars are pulling into the lounge. The customer, manager, and attorney are confused when the cops arrive at the lounge. They all claim to have not called the police. The police announce my name over the loudspeaker from the car, telling me not to move or they will have no choice but to shoot. Is this a prank? Thank God my attorney is here to document everything; I have no clue as to why I am being arrested. One police officer steps out of the car and instructs me to put my hands up as he reads my *Miranda Warning*. I keep silent the entire time and don't drop one bead of sweat. I have not committed a crime in over ten years, so I know they have the wrong person. This has to be some "Set It Off" mistake because this feels like a scene from a horror film. I know the law thinks that all Blacks look alike, but I am not incriminating myself.

"Your stupid ass left your ID on the floor. You were asking for this!" I know it's a setup because I don't even know where my ID is, but as soon as I find out who is behind this, I will take care of them.

When we arrive at the police station, the detective is waiting for me in the interrogation room. He'll be sadly mistaken when he realizes that I am just as clueless as he is about the entire 'crime.'

"Finally! You have made it easy for us to throw your ass in the slammer! This has been a long time coming, Mr. Jennings."

"I'm sorry; you've got the wrong man because I didn't rob no damn bank!"

"Since you want to have a blonde moment, we're going to tell your simple ass why you're here and show you the footage from your crime. You are under arrest for armed bank robbery and attempted murder. You even left the one piece of evidence that proves you are guilty." He tosses my ID on the table and says that I imprisoned myself.

"I own a top-notch lounge in the A, why the fuck would I rob a bank?! And attempted murder? Every time a Black man tries to make a living the legal way, 5-0 always pins a brotha down. This shit is a trap, but you aren't going to get me caught up."

The detective's eyes are filled with fury, and his skin is as red as the devil. Whoever is trying to set me up will have hell to pay once I get out of this hell hole. "Save the 'I Have a Dream' speech for another day because we have video evidence of you demanding the money and shooting that guard in the chest!"

Before I could utter a response, Tristan bursts in, creating a thicker tension inside of the room. "My client does not have anything further to say, as a matter of fact, where is the warrant for his arrest? There is none because he is innocent! I was with him on the day of the bank robbery, and I have proof."

The detective is even more infuriated at the audacity of Tristan. His stature can be quite intimidating, especially since he is 6'5, dark as midnight blue, and weighs at least 300 pounds. His work speaks for itself; he is the current day Johnnie Cochran. The detective locks the door and proceeds to play the video of the crime scene. "Oh, really? We'll see about that after we all view the footage! Maybe you were an accomplice, especially since he did not drive himself from the crime scene. You see that! The same height, build, and walk! Do you people think that you can fool technology? I think not!"

Tristan turns to me with a look of disappointment and hurt; he thinks I've betrayed him. I am almost in tears; this shit is fucking up my character and reputation!

"Sir, my client is innocent, and by the looks of it, your evidence does not show the victim's face nor are there any fingerprints that match his. Have you even checked the fingerprints on the doors, countertops and the ID? My client and I will be leaving until we are presented with a warrant for his arrest."

As we are walking out, he whispers in my ear, "If you did this shit then I will make sure your ass is six feet under. I don't know what mess you've gotten into, but it's not like you to do some underhanded shit and not tell me about it."

"I was with you the day of the robbery, and I make more money than the money that was stolen in the robbery. Why would I fuck up everything that I worked so hard for? You think I want to risk my family, life savings, and entire livelihood for some petty ass bank robbery?"

"You were with me the afternoon of the robbery, remember? You were reviewing the papers for the DNA test." "Exactly! You right, so you think you can get me off?" I can tell he is getting stressed already, I'm not worried though, because I'm innocent. "Let's see; you left my office at 2:30 pm and the bank robbery took place at 3:00 pm. There is no way you could have made it in time to rob a bank on that side of town. Could someone be trying to frame you? I can't even lie, the footage resembles you too well, and the ID is yours. Something is not right, Mr. Jennings, and we're going to get the truth."

"No, not anyone I can think of." Then it hit me. "The only person who has a vendetta against me is Chris, and he is also the only one who can successfully plant evidence against me. His lifelong dream is to see me rot in this motherfucker. But I already told you I'm going to off him as soon as those results come back. I'm telling you the truth, T. You're the last person I would lie to. You're the only one who can keep my record clean despite all the dirty shit I do. But I can assure you; I had nothing to do with that bank robbery." "You think Chris did this?" Tristan asks in shock. "I know he did, but we need proof."

"Look, they've got heavy evidence on you. I'm going to figure this shit out. You may have to sit in jail for two weeks until the arraignment, but whatever you do, don't say shit to anybody. I have a few friends in the system; Chris isn't the only one who can play dirty. My right-hand man is a judge in this district and owes me a favor. This case may be the one that makes me Partner in the firm. In the meantime, I'm going to get the footage and figure out who your stunt-double is. Don't say a word to anyone about this, not even to Jasmine. One slip of the tongue and you could end up in jail for the rest of your life."

Chapter 7: Jasmine

I Can't Stand the Rain

When it rains it not only pours, it monsoons. My husband and I can't seem to catch a break! I know that all these trials are happening so that we can strengthen our marriage, family, and businesses. As my Daddy would say, if it's not worth fighting for, then it's not worth having. *Antonio and I will win.* We are a winning team, especially with Tristan defending us. He's the best attorney in the state and has become like family to us. So, as soon as he called to tell me that my husband was being arrested, I knew that I didn't have to worry. It surely can't be over some bullshit seafood allegations. I speed race to the lounge, weaving through traffic as if there were a pregnant woman in my car delivering a baby. As soon as I arrive at the scene.

"Miss, are you related to the owner of the lounge?" A baritone voice cracked my thoughts, and I aggressively turn around and snap at him. "I am the co-owner of the lounge, Mrs. Jennings, Antonio's wife. Do you know what is going on—why was he arrested? My husband is not a criminal!" The detective looks at me as if I am lying. "I'm sure he's just as innocent as O.J., but until he's proven innocent by the law, he will remain in jail. The law has reason to believe that he robbed a bank for $100,000, as well as attempted to murder the security guard. Before you tell me that you know he is innocent, evidence proves otherwise."

He shows me a zip-lock bag that enclosed Antonio's ID; I have no clue what is happening, but I will defend my husband until the end of time. Antonio has a lot of explaining to do. I remain silent.

"Furthermore, MRS. JENNINGS, we have reason to believe that this lounge is a cover-up for fraudulent activity. We have a court-ordered warrant to perform an internal investigation on all your computers. We need to ensure that all of your data, funding, and other logistics are traced to a legal source."

Though my voice is shaking, I retaliate, "Is that why he is under arrest? I can assure you that everything about this lounge is 100 percent legal."

"Unfortunately, the law doesn't operate off your assurance. The FBI's Cyber Division is already en route."

An assembly of six cars barricaded the lounge; each car was guarded by an armed officer strapped in bulletproof gear. The detective advised me to step aside and cooperate unless I was willing to be my husband's cellmate. The other officers barge into the lounge, disassemble the cords from the wall, and remove every computer. They also asked for our accountant's information. I pant and tremble as they destroy the life that my husband and I worked so hard to build. I keep my composure, hold my tears, and let them do their job. I try not to think too hard about it; thankfully, Tristan calls to give me more details.

"Hey, Tristan, how soon can I see him? What's the exact date of his arraignment? The FBI is here so I can't say too much. I need to see my husband as soon as possible."

"About that, Mrs. Jennings, Antonio's arraignment isn't set until four weeks from today. The FBI cyber audit must be rendered before I can represent him in court. But to be honest with you, I don't think Antonio robbed any bank. We believe that Chris has something to do with this." "Chris? Is that even possible? I know that Chris wants to bring us down, but I don't think he'd stoop this low." "I'll have my forensics team analyze the video and investigate the voice. We'll win the case." "Thanks, Tristan. I'll call you later."

Tariq pulls up to the curb of the lounge. The FBI cars are still here causing a big scene; people are driving slowly and sticking their necks out of their windows. Nosey ass people who can't mind their own business are my pet peeve. "Hey sis, what's the 411?"

I burst into tears; I can't hold them any longer. I can't believe how vulnerable I am with my brother-in-law. Maybe because he reminds me of Antonio. I swear they're twins; the only difference is Tariq has a dark mole right under his eye. I sit in the passenger's seat and weep uncontrollably.
"Baby girl, what's wrong? Don't worry, Antonio will be out soon. I'm going to hold you down. If there's anything you need, and I mean ANYTHING, remember I am here for you."

He wipes my tears away then caresses my face. I try my best not to orgasm, although my panties are wetter than Niagara Falls. I straighten my back, exhale, and tell him what's going on. I know I need to be careful about what I mention because Antonio doesn't completely trust his brother.

"Antonio was arrested for a bank robbery that happened a couple of weeks ago. But I know he didn't do that shit. You have to help me hold the lounge down; the FBI is auditing all of our computers, so we're closed until further notice."

"Ok, I got you, sis. Whatever you need, I'm here. Antonio gave me a little insight on how to run the lounge." "Thank you; I appreciate you stepping up to the plate. You are truly your brother's keeper. I got to go, Ty. I'm going to check on Antonio. I'll meet you at the house later this evening."

The sexual tension between Tariq and I is painstakingly thick. I don't like to be alone with him for too long, so this is a perfect time to break loose.

I arrive at the jail, only to find the front desk vacant. The grungy, off-white walls block any sunlight that may be emitted from the tinted windows. The waiting room reeks of urine, and everyone looks just as hopeless as me. I wait a few minutes, and finally, an older lady asks if she can assist me. I told her why I was there, and she informed me that Antonio wasn't receiving visitors now.

"Not receiving visitors. I am his wife! Why is he restricted from visitation?"

"Your guess is better than mine, Mrs. Jennings. I'm sorry that you can't see your husband." My blood is boiling, but I refuse to act out of character and embarrass Antonio. Surprisingly, as I am exiting Chris is entering the waiting room. "What the hell are you doing here? Did you have something to do with my husband's arrest?" He smirks and acts clueless. "I don't know why your thug husband got arrested. All I know is that the test results will be in soon!" "Go to hell, Chris!"

"I guess you're Bonnie and he's Clyde, huh? Look, Mrs. Clyde, I'm getting custody of my son whether you like it or not. I don't know if you've forgotten, but I am the law. You're letting some thug criminal raise my boy and..." I cut him off and slap the shit out of him. My hand imprint is embedded in his face; his cheek is swollen and turning red. "Next time I'm dotting your eye if you mention my family!" I go to the bathroom to calm down. My phone rings, it's my Mama. "Hey, baby girl, what's going on?" I exclaimed, "Mom, everything is going downhill! I am so lost and overwhelmed."

"I think I know how to brighten your day." She puts my babies on the phone, and as soon as I hear their voices, I can't help but smile. We say our 'I love you's' and I tell them to put Grandma on the phone. "Jasmine, I didn't raise a quitter. You've got this! Boss up and handle your business like a woman. Don't let Chris bully you. Aunt Janice is calling; love you, bye." As I am leaving the bathroom, I run into the detective who is representing Antonio's case. "You caught me at the right time, Mrs. Jennings." He escorts me to a private conference room in the back and asks a series of questions about how the business receives funding. I assured him that my husband didn't rob a bank, let alone attempt to murder a guard. I told him that we own property in Atlanta and used the revenue to fund the lounge. He was listening intently, amazed at how well I was able to trace the fund for every expense. "Mrs. Jennings, I am quite impressed with how organized you are. After assessing your finances, everything seems to be legitimate. Your lounge grossed a million dollars last year, so I'm quite sure $100,000 is petty cash for Mr. Jennings. However, in order to complete the investigation, I'll need you to bring me an affidavit, bill of sale, and other legal documents stating that you own properties. After that, all charges will be expunged. I am also working with Mr. Banks to exonerate Mr. Jennings from fraud charges. He is still being charged for the bank robbery and attempted murder until further notice."

Chapter 8: Tariq

Time to Right My Wrongs

My conscience has finally gotten the best of me, so I decided to confess to Antonio, no matter the repercussions. I need to man the fuck up and let my brother know that Chris was the mastermind behind his demise, while I was used as a puppet. Truth be told, I am no better than Chris, especially since I went through with the steps to frame my brother. Ever since Antonio's arrest, I have not been able to sleep without waking up in cold sweats; my pillows and sheets are drenched in guilt. Last night I had a dream that my mirror's reflection was Judas from the bible. What good is my freedom if it costs the betrayal, incarceration, and torment of my flesh and blood?

I can't front; my brother is one hell of a businessman; I have no clue how he manages a family, employees, and remains the most popular nightlife hub in metro-Atlanta. His lounge grosses at least $4,000 per day, not counting tips. It's a lot of work; I'm usually in the lounge from 9 am to 2 am each day. I never realized how much of a real man my brother is; instead, I was selfishly thinking of ways to destroy him. I'm the one who should be incarcerated or buried 6-feet under for the sneak shit I just pulled. I know that the consequence of crossing Antonio is death and at this point, I feel like a dead man walking. I have tried to contact Chris for at least three days, but his bitch ass is ignoring my phone call. What can I expect from a snake-like him? Jasmine has been an emotional wreck, their children have been calling for Antonio almost every day, and I have been doing my best to hold down the lounge. I can tell that Jasmine wants me to console her by the way that she walks around the house. Yesterday she asked me if I could unzip her dress, which stopped at the lower part of her torso. I brushed my hand down her waist, and she blurted a moan that sounded like an orgasm. She constantly walks around the house in booty shorts; sometimes she cooks breakfast in her bra and pretends like she didn't realize that she was topless. But I respect my brother's boundaries and don't give in to temptation. If Jasmine keeps trying me though, she just may get what she's asking for. Although she's low-key flirting with me, that doesn't take away from the fact that she is distraught about my brother's circumstance.

"Damn, Tariq!" I yell to myself. How did I let myself get this desperate for freedom? At first, I was mad at my brother for cutting me off while I was in prison, I'll admit I was feeling entitled to his half of the money. But after learning the facts about my brother's struggle to create a happy life and witnessing how difficult it is to be in his shoes, I feel like a pile of shit. I haven't eaten in three days because the guilt has taken away my appetite. I attempt to contact Chris one more time before I go to confess to Antonio, and of course, he doesn't answer. As I was getting ready, I attempted to call Chris one more time to give him a heads up, but he rejects my call for the hundredth time. I am not begging a grown man to answer my phone call, so, if he wants to suffer the wrath of Antonio after he's released from jail, then that's on him.

I muster the strength to visit Antonio in the rotten facility that he now calls home until further notice. I always imagined avenging my brother for neglecting me while I was in prison, but now I feel like the lesser human being. The walls inside of the jail are designed with asbestos, the floors are creaky, and the waiting area smells like halitosis and other unidentifiable scents. I sign my name on the waiting list for visitation. "Mr. Tariq Jennings, you got lucky. We just granted him visitation today. Are you a blood relative?"

"Yes, I am his brother."

"Great, he could use a brother right about now. He's been locked in the library day in and day out. He even got a pair of glasses and acts as if Malcolm X is his dad. I'll grab him for you. At first glance, I thought you were the same person!" My heart plummeted to my stomach after she stated the obvious—my brother and I *could* be the same person; damn, I am worse than Chris. Antonio has a shocking reaction once he realizes it's me. The dull, scratched glass that separates us makes it challenging to communicate. I decided that I am getting this off my chest despite the communication barrier. "Damn, you're the last person I expected to see. How's my wife? Is everything ok with the lounge?" I respond by bowing my head in shame. Jasmine must have softened him because I can tell that he is much more temperate these days.

"Everyone is doing well, but that is not why I came to visit today. There's something I need to get off of my chest, Ant." He arches one eyebrow and squints his eyes in confusion. My tone is aggressive, but Antonio doesn't flinch. "Man, listen, I was miserable when I was in prison! You stopped the attorney from working on my case, there were no more visits nor was there any money on my books. I felt betrayed by the person who I trusted the most." He rubs his temples in distress. "So, what does that have to do with me or my situation? What did you come down here for, Ty?" "A lawyer appeared out of nowhere saying he wanted to help me out, claiming that he would legally exonerate me from all of my charges. His name is Chris, and he told me that to get my freedom, I had to frame you. I didn't have any other options, Ant. I was desperate as fuck. But now I am regretting it all. I was fucked up, Antonio! I'm sorry man." He is silent for a second then punches the glass. I am in tears, shit, this is the first time I've cried in 20 years. The guard tells him to calm down, or his visitation will end.

"What the fuck do you mean? My flesh and blood framed me? You were the one on the camera? Damn, my ID did go missing after you moved in. I can't believe you sold out your brother for $100,000, damn bruh." He leans closer to the glass and whispers, "You know I can have your ass dead within 24 hours, and nobody would suspect a thing, as well as your accomplice." I am sweating bullets, and my heart could leap out my skin at any moment. "Bro, I—" "I am not your brother." "Look, all I am saying is that I did not realize how evil this man was, nor did I know the extent to which he hurt Jasmine. How was I supposed to know all of the family business? It's not like you even told me you got married, had two kids, started a business, you ain't tell me shit. You're right; I guess we aren't brothers. Fuck it! Jasmine said some shit I won't forget; she said, 'You are your brother's keeper.' Chris has been blackmailing me ever since we did the robbery, and I can't take it anymore. I'm willing to right my wrong even if it means losing my life." He's quiet for a moment, wipes a tear from his eyes, and looks up at me with fury. "You damn right, you're going to right your wrong. Death would be too easy. I have something else in mind." He instructs me to go along with the plan that Chris devised and pretend as if Antonio does not know a thing.

"I'm going to consult with my attorney, Tristan, in the morning."

"What about Chris? What if he tries to send me back to jail after he realizes you know the plan?" The look of anger comes back, and he says, "You don't have to worry about him, it's over for him. But don't you say a word." Antonio slams the phone on the receiver and storms to his cell. My conscience is clear, but I am scared as shit for Chris and myself. No matter what happens, my brother knows where my loyalty lies. Chris is a snake. He doesn't mean shit to me, as a matter of fact, it is time for me to prove my loyalty to Antonio and do all that can to get him out of jail.

I drive back home, so Jas isn't worried about their family car. They have a nice ass Cadillac ATS, and my flexing ass is hype as shit to be whippin' it. The drive home clears my mind from the millions of thoughts that are distracting me. What will Chris do once he finds out? What is Antonio going to do to both of us? This shit is just too much. I can't wait until Tristan knows the truth, hopefully, then, we can take Chris ass out. It is family over everything no matter what.

Chapter 9: Antonio

It All Comes to An End

"All rise. Docket B67-5623. Jennings v. The City of Atlanta. The Court is now in session. Please be seated." I can't believe that I am once again on the wrong side of the justice system. The judge has a dismissive look on his face as he sifts through my case. He smirks at Tristan in a way that tells me that he has already sentenced my fate in his head. Chris doesn't realize that this not only fucks up my record but the reputation of all Black men. Of course, Chris thinks he is above the law, but as soon as Tristan gets me out of here, he will regret the day he was born. My brother's desperate need to be released from jail almost cost me a lifetime in prison. My freedom is in the hands of Tristan's ability to prove to the judge that I am innocent. I have faith that I will beat the case, but Tristan just needs to mention Chris' blackmail, which is a crime under state law. Chris ignited a flame that has spiraled into a wildfire that will destroy his very existence. Not only has he tainted my brother, but now he is coming after my son, UNACCEPTABLE. It is a miracle that Tristan was able to secure a court date within a month of me getting booked. I do not doubt that he will be able to get me out of this hell-hole. I haven't spoken to Jasmine in about two weeks, and I am going insane! The timbre of her voice is ingrained in my head and is the only comfort that I have had in my moment of solitude in jail. I don't bother to tell her about the court date because I don't want to instill false hopes of my freedom. At this point, God is the only intercessor who can vindicate me.

Tristan motions to speak on my behalf. "Your Honor, please consider my client's excellent behavior since he's been in jail, plus he has proof that the financial records from his club are legitimate. I understand that the person who robbed the bank has a striking resemblance to Mr. Jennings, but my client has no motive to rob a bank for such a meager amount of money. He has a family, a successful, legal business, and is trying his best to escape the troughs of a criminal lifestyle. I am aware that cases like his may slide across your desk every day, but please consider his record. He has only committed misdemeanors, most of which were not money-related. Your Honor, my client was framed." The judge raises his brows in agitation and adjusts his glasses.

"Mr. Banks, how do you explain the dropped identification? While I can see that the evidence is subpar and insufficient, I am led to believe that it was Mr. Jennings who robbed the bank, based on the footage from the videotape."

"Your Honor, I have brought the financial records that prove how he earns income; I was even able to re-examine the footage where we can see that there is height difference in my client and the person who is framing him. I also have a written testament of his character from one of his investors." The judge analyzes the film, reads the letter and removes his glasses from his face. He begins to rub his temple while he gathers his thoughts frustratingly. "Mr. Banks, it is unorthodox for me to release a person after the first trial. However, I am astoundingly moved by his letter of character and the legitimacy of his business's records. I am granting Mr. Jennings an early release. My office will be in communication with you to complete the process. I don't expect to see you in my courtroom ever again, Mr. Jennings.

As for you Mr. Banks, I think you have the power to man this bench one day, don't let me down. Mr. Jennings, I am placing you on a 72-hour house arrest so that my team and I can keep track of your whereabouts. If you step foot outside of the court-ordered radius, then I will personally send law enforcement to arrest you. This is not only your second chance, but it is also your last chance! Next time I see you in my courtroom you better have tangible evidence proving that you are innocent!"

I hug Tristan and nod to the judge to express my immense gratitude. My eyes are filled with tears of joy, and all I can think about is my baby, Jasmine. I call her five times but no answer, she probably has her hands tied in the lounge. Tristan and I head to his office so that I can get myself together. Since my brother does not mind setting people up, I'm sure he will be more than willing to get his hands dirty while we handle Chris. "What the hell is going on, Antonio? You're out of jail, but we still need to have the case expunged. Is there anything else I need to know?" I tell him about my brother and Chris setting me up, the blackmail, the DNA test, and my plan to kill Chris. Chris is one dumb ass motherfucka! Did he think my brother wouldn't let me in on this shit? Snakes always show their venom, but his ass won't be biting anyone else anytime soon. Tristan was so stoked that he slammed the breaks in the middle of traffic. "What the fuck do you mean your brother framed you? I need to know all of the details of your plan for Chris. One mistake and your ass is in prison for the rest of your life, and there will be nothing I can do about it. At least your brother was brave enough to confess to you; you know he has always admired you to a fault." "I am not going to front, bruh, this shit hurt me to my core. First, he came after Jasmine, then my only brother, now he's abusing his power as an attorney to take my son. It's only so much I can take. This man has been knocking on death's door for a long time; he will finally have his chance to meet the other side." When we arrive at his office, he instructs his assistant to void all of his meetings and close the office for the day. She can tell that he is not in the mood to offer any explanation for his sudden requests. He tells her to take the day off early. This is rare, so she complies with no question. "Thank you, Mr. Banks. See you on Monday." "Please set the alarm and lock all of the doors behind you; thank you."

He pours us both a drink before pulling out a stack of confidential files. "We are planning this shit out together, Antonio. In order to save your ass, I need to know every single plan. This is a dead man walking." I have never seen Tristan this gutter; it is good to know that he is loyal to my family. As soon as this shit blows over, I am cutting him a big ass check.

"Check it; we are going to wire my brother so we can record all of his conversations with Chris. We may even get the wire that has the mini-cam concealed in it. He won't suspect a thing. He enjoys bragging about how well he set me up and put my brother against me. The joke is on this clown."

Tristan is writing notes and researching some legal information just in case anything should go wrong. He says that once we prove that Chris set me up and blackmailed Tariq, he can begin the process to exonerate my charges and expunge them from my record.

"What about the papers, Ant? The DNA test, has it come back yet? That shit he pulled in North Carolina was against the law, too." "No, they haven't. Honestly, I don't give a damn about any papers. Jr. is my son! I was there when he was born, and I am the only father that he knows. Chris has me fucked up if he thinks that I am about to let him ruin MY SON'S life!" My blood is boiling, and Tristan can see the rage in my eyes. I should be blaming Claire for this, she's the one who cheated on me, tortured Jasmine, and made all of our lives a living hell. Claire stopped having sex with me because she was too busy fucking him. That's in the past though, and soon enough, Chris will be a past thought.

"Is there a legal way to make Chris disappear without a trace? Will the court suspect anything? I need our plan to be seamless."

"Technically speaking, no, the court has no motive to suspect that you had anything to with his sudden disappearance. The court doesn't even know that your brother framed you or that Chris violated the law while releasing Tariq from prison. We can stage it as if he skipped to Cuba. As for Tariq, I can ask the court to grant him immunity, citing that he was forced to frame you under Chris manipulation and plus he is being a productive citizen. Now if Tariq does anything, anything as simple as driving with a missing tail light, then his ass is back in prison for life, under maximum security."

"Say no more, boss. Can you give me a lift home? I've been trying to reach Jas for hours now, and she's still not answering." "No problem, but remember, this plan stays between the two of us. All Jasmine needs to know is that you handled it. If there are too many heads involved, then the whole shit is over for us all. Got it?"

"Thank you; you are the definition of a real friend."

Chapter 10: Jasmine

Please Forgive Me

I have been wallowing in a sorrowful solitude for the past month due to Antonio's incarceration. I can't sleep, have lost 10 pounds, and the only place where I can find slight joy is in the lounge. Tariq and I have built up a sexual tension that seems impossible to break. My emotions are in disarray, Tariq is walking on eggshells, my children want to talk to Daddy, and I have not had sex in a month. Antonio and I usually get in seven to eight times a week, so, it feels like I have been living in the Sahara Desert since he's been in jail. My days have been filled with nothing but Sauvignon Blanc every day. I can't go to sleep without crying; I've never been apart from Antonio this long, and it's killing me. Tariq is not making it any easier to resist his sexy ass, especially since he takes it upon himself to check on me throughout the day, make sure I eat at least one meal a day, and walks around half-naked effortlessly flexing his muscles and flashing tattoos. He is a listening ear, a natural comforter and is willing to do whatever he has to so that I can sleep easier. I can't betray my husband, but what am I to do in this situation? I haven't heard from Antonio since I went there and couldn't see him in jail. I am in a frenzy that has no escape.

"Jas, are you ok? Do you need anything while I'm out? I see that you are almost out of your fancy wine." I try to speak but instead a tear rolls from my eye. He rushes to me and buries my head in his chest. My tears streamed down my face and drenched his shirt. "Ty, I can't do this anymore, I can feel myself breaking down. I can't do this alone; it's too much.

The stress is killing me. I think you're the only one who I can trust." "Jas, I have something to tell you. I am not as innocent as you think. I'm the reason that Antonio is locked up." Tears begin to flood my eyes again, speechless, I let him finish his speech. "A few months ago, Chris came to me in prison and gave me an offer I couldn't pass up. I was still holding a grudge toward my brother for neglecting me in the penitentiary. I thought he was out here living the lavish life while I was rotting in that shit-hole. So, I thought this was a perfect opportunity to avenge Antonio for making me suffer. Chris made it seem so easy—all I'd have to do was frame Ant as a bank robber, and I'd be free for good. But I didn't realize that this shit was set up to put Ant and me against one another. All Chris cares about is taking your son and killing Antonio. I'm sorry, Jas. I've already told all of this Antonio." After everything that I have been through this is just the icing on the cake. At least he manned up about it. In a weird way, his confession draws me closer to him. He pours us both a shot of Hennessy, then commands the entertainment system to play my favorite Temptations song, *Just My Imagination*. "This really is my imagination, Jas. I wish I had the badass wife, beautiful children and super-successful businesses that bring in a half a million dollars every year." "It's not too late, Ty. You can have all of this and more. You have righted your wrong, I'm sure you'll find happiness and—" As he leans in to kiss me, I hear a key turning in the door—it's Antonio! "Baby! Why didn't you tell me you were coming home?" "Well, I've been calling you all day, but your phone has been going straight to voicemail." I can't believe the one time that Ty and I kiss, my husband catches us! His voice starts to break.

"So you fucking my brother! I get to come home to see my

brother and my wife having a rendezvous? What the fuck you playing slow jams and taking shots for? You don't even drink this much with me around, are you fucking kidding me? I know I didn't just see this bullshit! I know I didn't." "No, Antonio, it's not what you think!" I yell at the top of my lungs. Tariq jumps in and tries to explain, but Antonio interrupts him by pushing him onto the couch. "Jasmine, take yo ass upstairs! Now!" I'm scared of all of our lives, so I do as I am told. I hear them go back and forth right before the front door slams shut.

Antonio storms upstairs with steam coming from his entire body. I have never been this afraid for my life. "I'm in jail for one month, one month! And I come home to find you entertaining my brother! Instead of preparing for my return, I find you half-dressed, slow dancing and taking shots like this is a damn party. You know good, and damn well you don't drink that much, especially when I'm not around. You know better than that, Jas. How can you betray me like that?" I feel so ashamed of my behavior that I don't know what to say.

I know that my tears will not change a thing, so I have to woman up to my actions. "Baby, I promise you we did not even kiss. This was the first time that anything like this has happened. Please, baby, don't be mad at him. It wasn't him; it was me. Please forgive me. I got so desperate while you were gone—I didn't have anyone to talk to, and Tariq was the only one here. He has nothing but respect for you. Baby, you know I wouldn't cross that line. Antonio, please hear me out!" I grab his hand; he yanks it back.

"Get off me! I can't believe you right now, yo!" He sits on our bed and sinks his head in his lap. He is not budging, so, I pull up the house camera on my phone. He installed hidden cameras all around the house just in case of emergencies. I play the footage so he can see everything, including what he walked into. As soon as he heard me crying and Ty confessing his wrongs, he looked up in relief. He kept replaying it to make sure it was nothing more than what he saw. Thankfully our lips didn't touch. He grabs a towel from the closet, goes straight to the bathroom and slams the door behind him.

I quickly undress and decide to accompany him in the shower. "Jas, I'm not dealing with you right now." He didn't notice that I had been standing there naked, yearning for his love right now. I step into the shower to ease his tension. He resists for a second and finally yields to me. "Jas, I see the footage. Are you sure that nothing else happened?"

"Positive, Antonio. I only love you. I have no reason to be dishonest."

He lifted me up and placed me on the wall of the shower, wrapped my legs around his waist and began to thrust every inch of his manhood into me. I am finally able to let all of my frustration out with my husband! "I'm sorry," I whisper in his ear, as he bites my shoulder blade. He goes deeper into my body as I accept every piece of him. We both climax and let the water cleanse our bodies. He holds me tightly and assures me that everything will be ok.

When we step out of the shower I notice the monitor bracelet on his ankle. "What's next?", I ask. "We have a plan, Tristan and I have everything mapped out, all I need you to do is to be with our babies, and everything will be fine." I don't ask any questions; I decide to let him handle it and work on being a better wife. "Jasmine, do you love me?" "Yes, why would you ever question my love for you?" "Jasmine, look at me. Stare into my eyes. Do you love me?" "Yes." " Do you trust me?" I gaze at him in confusion, wondering why he keeps asking me the same question. I replied, "Yes baby. You don't even have to ask me that." He embraced me in a tight hug and said if anything was to ever happen to him the kids and I are set for life.

Chapter 11: Tariq

Time to Make This Right

The chirping birds are the only ones happy to be up at the crack of dawn, not to mention the roosters who woke a brotha up before the sun could fully set. The fog blocks my view of the sun; this shit reminds me of all of the years I prayed to see the sun but wasn't allowed to. Back then, the only fog blocking the sun was a tall ass barbed wire fence. The annoying ass birds are forcing me to wake up earlier than I would like, but hell, the sooner I cut Chris off, the better. It feels good to set this clown up, especially since he blackmailed me into setting up my flesh and blood. No longer will I be his do-boy and little puppet, his revenge will be served as cold as a block of ice. Chris will regret the day he visited me in prison. As soon as I jump out of bed, I hear three knocks on the door; it must be Tristan. He is here bright and early, fully dressed, and ready to wire my ass up. My stomach turns as I walk to the door because I am afraid that Chris will find out I'm wired. My head is bursting bullets, and my palms are wetter than a drenched mop. Tristan can tell that I am nervous about framing Chris, so he breaks the ice with a shot of Hennessy. I throw that shit back like its water and suddenly my mind becomes mellow. I always looked down on cats who wore wires because that's the lowest form of snitching. But, considering the mayhem that Chris caused, he deserves jail. All that remorseful shit is for the birds; I can't have him fucking my family over. Tristan chimes in to ease my frustration about the situation.

"Relax, man; the law is going to cover you. All you have to do is get him to tell on himself. Let him do most of the talking, especially since he is proud of framing Ant. Ask him to run down the entire plan, word for word, so we can add every piece to the puzzle. Listen, Ty, what goes around comes around; I hope Chris is prepared to eat the same shit he has fed everyone else."

"Man, you're right. I can't wait until that filthy maggot is behind bars. I've never met such a hateful, pitiful person in all my years on earth. Once I bring up Antonio's name this man gets diarrhea of the mouth."

Tristan wires the transmitter to my chest and places a small device in his pocket. He brings us both a pair of Bluetooth headphones. The headphones are in sync with the transmitter and the device that Tristan has to track my location. I can't believe I have to go to such an extreme measure for Chris to confess. At the end of the day, this is real freedom—righting my wrongs so that the culprit can serve his time. Sure enough, at 9:00 on the dot Chris is blowing my phone up demanding to know where I am. I tell him that I am on the way, little does he know the feds are with me.

"Tristan, let me go meet this bum ass boy. This shouldn't take any more than an hour at the max. I'll catch an Uber home."

When I arrive at his house, I can tell that he has been drinking heavily and completely neglected his health and home. Walking through his grass is like walking through a forest; the grass is as tall as me, and his house looks abandoned. Flies greeted me at the door, the front window is shattered, and the door seems like it will fall off of the hinges if anyone closes it too hard. Chris is already living in a mental prison because he can't let go of the past. But none of that shit is phasing me because I have to mend my relationship with Antonio. Chris is sitting on the front porch with a bottle of Grey Goose on his left side and a bottle of Bacardi on his right; his eyes are bloodshot red.

He angrily shouts at me, "Why the fuck did you not tell me Antonio was released from jail or that Tristan Banks is his attorney? I will have both of your asses locked up with the quickness, Tariq!"

"Listen, you didn't ask, and I don't volunteer unnecessary information. Remind me of what is supposed to be happening here. What was the initial deal that we agreed on when you bailed me out of jail? I want to make sure I am maintaining my end of the bargain."

"That's typical; you would forget your part after I set you free. The deal was for you to rob the bank, give me the dough, leave Antonio's ID at the scene, and make sure he never sees the light of day. My question to you is, how the fuck did this man get out so quickly? Tristan's ass isn't that good, and I know you don't have any bail money, so what's up?"

"Oh, yeah, you're right. I did all of that; I don't know how the hell Antonio got out because that's none of my business."

The more he drinks, the more infuriated he becomes and attempts to take his anger out on me by aggressively grabbing my arm. I yanked away from his grip and push him back onto the porch. I should punch him dead in his chest, but that would send him to the hospital and me to prison for life. The last time I jabbed someone in the chest I broke their entire rib cage.

"Chris, you got one more damn time to touch me, and I'm going to beat your ass mercilessly. Whatever beef you have with my brother you can take that up with him. I did your dirty work; the rest is up to you." He shot me a look of pity and defeat; too bad my sympathy card is invalid.

"My bad man, I'm so fucking stressed out I don't know what to do. I know I can't take this shit out on you when it's Antonio who has fucked up my life. He has taken fatherhood away from me, and for that, I am making sure his ass has a permanent residency in jail. I only needed you to frame him so I could build up a case with substantial evidence. After his criminal ass is locked up, I can get my family back. Jasmine is supposed to be my wife. That was supposed to be my son. I'm not worried about the results of the DNA test; I know Jr. is mine. As a matter of fact, after I receive full custody of my son, I am renaming him." He looks so desperate and lifeless. I hate to be the bearer of bad news, but Jasmine is not leaving my brother so, Chris has to accept reality.

"Listen, bro, Jasmine is never leaving Ant, you better believe that. What good will it do you to get Jasmine back in your bed anyway? The picture-perfect family that you created in your mind does not exist. I think you should move the hell on with your life. Was her pussy so good that you're building a case against her husband? That's some sick shit, yo." He takes a large gulp of the Bacardi and then throws it into the only window that had a full set of glass in it.

"No, Tariq, you listen to me! Antonio is going to suffer just as much as I have, even worse because I'm sending his ass to the filthiest prison in America, Rikers Island! See, I knew you and Antonio weren't on good terms, so it was easy to include you in my plan. The fact that you are his blood brother makes revenge even sweeter. Do you think I give a fuck about Jasmine wanting to take me back? Fuck her too, all I care about is raising my son. If that means framing Antonio every day of the week, then that is exactly what I will do." His eyes water up, but just before he sheds a tear, he downs the last bit of Grey Goose that was left in the bottle. I smirk and look around at the chaos that he lives in. Hell, even prison wasn't this polluted.

"Damn, Chris, my brother really has you rattled, huh?"

"You don't get it, do you? He stole my first-born son!"

I try to rationalize with him.

"He wasn't the one who started any of this shit. You and his ex-wife were sneaking around, so you both had to suffer the consequences. Antonio is a ruthless motherfucker. I'm surprised he didn't kill your ass when he offed your little concubine. All my brother did was scoop Jasmine up when she needed it the most. Clearly, you didn't give a damn about losing her back then. Stop this woe is me bullshit. No one wants to hear you cry about how 'he took my girl.' She's a grown woman who is married to a grown man, which is my brother. Accept it and move the fuck on."

"Fuck you, Tariq! I should have let your ass rot in prison and found someone else to help me bring Antonio down. I don't give a shit about what you're saying, the DNA test will prove what Jasmine and I both know I am his father! Jasmine nor Chris will ever see my son ever again in life!" His phone rings, so he goes inside to take the call privately. I realized his briefcase was sitting by his chair, open and disheveled with papers. I spot a manila envelope labeled DNA Diagnostic Center. I peeked inside the doorway to ensure he was still on the phone. I grab the envelope, fluff his papers around, so it doesn't look suspicious and hit my Uber ride up and head home. This shit was easier than taking candy from a baby.

Hopefully, this will make things right between my brother and me, especially since he walked in on Jasmine and me. Thank goodness we didn't actually kiss! My Uber arrives as soon as Chris comes back to the porch. I holler out the window, "I got shit to do, you don't need me anymore, you need a psychiatrist!"

Chapter 12: Antonio

Final Ruling

The judge has proven that the pen is mightier than the sword, but I am ready to slit Chris' neck on sight due to the tragedy he has caused my family. First, he started with my wife, then attempted to corrupt my brother, and now he is trying to kidnap my first-born child, the only person who will carry my legacy. If he thought I was evil a few years ago, he would be able to experience the dire wrath that awaits him in a few days. I can't front though, the suspense is killing me, I've lost at least 15 pounds in the last two months, and clumps of hair are falling out by the day. A few of my employees even had the audacity to ask me how chemotherapy was going—how do I explain that the cancer is my wife's ex-boyfriend? Chris' evilness has infiltrated every aspect of my life, and the only way to solve the problem is to lay him to rest permanently. Honestly, I could give two fucks about a DNA test because Jr. is my son!

My home office is the only refuge that I have right now, especially since the Feds seized our computers and other equipment. This situation has blown my life to smithereens, and every time I attempt to pick up one piece, something else crumbles. The business has been incredibly slow, and neither Jasmine nor I have been able to get back into the swing of things. Jasmine has not had the time to focus on the lounge in North Carolina because she's too depressed to admit that the one in Atlanta is falling apart. Her parents have been extremely helpful and compassionate, but I can tell they are ready for our babies to come home. They don't have to worry too much longer; after this Chris shit over, we'll be able to resume business as usual.

Tristan has been a God-send during this time; he even persuaded the judge to extend the house arrest while we continue to search for tangible evidence that proves I am innocent. Chris has a heavy ransom on his head for fucking up my family. I am going to collect everything that was stolen from me, including my wife's heart. At this point I don't know what to think or how to feel, Jasmine has never lied to me, so when she says nothing happened between her and Ty, I believe her. On the other hand, my eyes did not deceive me. But now is not the time to get distracted by that bullshit, we have bigger fish to fry and can't quarrel over frivolous shit. It was Chris who blackmailed my brother and dangled a taste of false freedom in his face. Shit, I can't say I would have acted any different if I were Ty, he had already spent ten years in the joint. I have to forgive my brother in order to live a happy life that Jasmine and I created together. Just as I was about to call Tristan, I heard a knock at the door. It can't be Jas because she never knocks.

"Come in." Tariq peeps his head inside the door, asking if we could chat for a bit.

"I guess we have brother's intuition because I was just thinking about you. What's up, little bro?"

"First, I want to apologize for the other night; it wasn't Jasmine's fault at all. I take full responsibility for taking advantage of Jasmine while she was in a vulnerable state. I swear nothing happened while you were booked, and I will never violate you again. Word is bond."

I walk past him, brushed my shoulder against his, and grab a piece of paper from my printer. Silence speaks volumes, and the tension in the room could be cut with a knife. I respect the fact that he doesn't make a move until I do; he doesn't sit until I look comfortable in my chair and doesn't speak until I speak first. I can respect the fact that he came back to clear the air.

"Big bro, I have something that might pique your interest." He waves the envelope with the DNA results in my face. I know what it is but fear that I may be devastated by the answers. The angst is blatant, and my body language says that I may suffer a panic attack at that very moment.

"I figured you might want to see it before Chris opened it." I stared at the envelope for a second, thinking back to how everything started with Chris, Jas, and Claire. "This whole situation has been one hot ass mess!" I vented to Tariq and felt my face heating by the minute.

I begin to reflect on the days when Jasmine was pregnant with Jr., and I become enraged at the thought of Chris raising my son.

"Man, you gotta understand, I was the one who rubbed Jas's feet during her pregnancy, was up with her during morning sickness. I cut his umbilical cord, not Chris!" I take a deep breath in and exhale a strong gust of wind. "Ty, that little boy means the world to me! He makes me want to be a better man every single day, and this devil is trying to take that away from me. I can't take this shit!"

My brother empathizes with my pain.

"He's the only father you know, and we're going to keep it that way." I let his words settle in my mind and thank God that I have my brother back.

"Ty, we had our issues, but I need you right now. You got my back?"

"Always bro, I got you; no questions asked."

"My man, 50 grand! Check it; I got Jasmine's cell so I can pretend like I am her. I am going to text Chris and ask him to come over so we can have a little chat."

I instructed Tariq to secure the envelope in my safe until Chris comes over in the morning.

"Ty, go ahead and grab all the supplies we'll need. It's go time." He shot me a look that solidified his role. I can't talk too much around Jasmine because I don't want her to freeze when shit pops off. It seems like tomorrow is an eternity, but at least we have the results. This test will change everyone's life for better or worse tomorrow morning.

Chapter 13: Antonio Part I

By Any Means Necessary

It's 7:30 a.m., and I have been on the phone with Jasmine for exactly two hours, reassuring her that if she plays her part, everything will be gravy. I have never had to involve her in my past life, but at this point, I don't have a choice. It is time for Chris to meet his fate, and I have no problem expediting the process.

"Baby, I need you to be on your best behavior and cooperate with me. If our plan is going to be successful, then I need you to be a team player. Everyone's position is vital and can either fuel the plan or fail it. Chris will be here in five minutes, so, I need you to stay on the phone with him the entire time he is driving over here. This is the only way we will be able to keep our family together." "You know I trust you, baby. I feel like this is all my fault since he is my ex-boyfriend. Do whatever you have to do to keep our family together. I love you."

Although Jasmine has a mountain of guilt on her back, this is totally Chris's fault, especially since he knows I don't play games about my family. He has been digging his own grave since the day he set foot on my in-laws' property and traumatized my son. The way I see it, his death is overdue justice that my family and the justice system deserve. Jasmine is at her parents' house until the deed is done; I did not want her to witness the atrocity that Chris is about to endure. She was happy to see the children and her mother, too. Jasmine deserves peace, as for me, I don't mind getting my hands dirty so that my family can live a happy life. After all, as the head of the house, it is vital that I protect them at all costs.

After I finished talking to Jasmine, I hear the doorbell ring; it's Tristan. This man is on time no matter what, I can appreciate that. He is insanely happy and lunged his arms at me as if I were his mother.

"Good morning, I caught an Uber here, so Chris won't suspect anything. On another note, guess who was able to persuade the judge to drop all of your charges? This guy here! I sent the recording to the District Attorney office, and they reasoned that the fingerprints did not match the objects submitted by the bank. I explained to them that Chris was the head honcho who blackmailed your brother, a vulnerable inmate, to rob a bank in exchange for permanent freedom. The State has issued a warrant for Chris's arrest. His license to practice law in the state of Georgia and North Carolina have both been revoked. In the mind of the law, it would make sense for him to skip town."

"Good shit. You're going to be one powerful judge, Tristan. All I can say is thank you. Ya boy should be here any minute now; he's on the phone with Jasmine. Tariq is in the backroom waiting for Chris to come through. Make sure your phones are on mute. Shit's about to go down."

Jasmine sends a text to inform me that Chris is five minutes away from our house. The beam of his headlights is blinding me at the window, so, I hide behind the door until it is time to open it. Jasmine is guiding him into the pitch-black house with the assumption that she is behind the door. He's smiling from ear to hear and does the secret knock that Jasmine has given him. I open the door swiftly, put him in a chokehold and knee him in the stomach until he coughs up blood.

"That little, conniving skank! I should have known you were behind this operation the whole time. You've already stolen my son, what next, my soul?" I pick him up from the ground and chain his wrists and ankles to a chair. His eyes are rolling to the back of his head so, I dump a bucket of water on him to wake his pitiful ass up. He finally comes to reality, begging to hear him out. "I don't give a fuck what you do to me; my legacy lives through MY SON. In case you were wondering, yes, I did bring the results to my test. I'll let you open Pandora's Box. How about you unchain me now, so, I can prove to you what we both already know."

"Really, now? We'll both find out right here, right now." As I wave the envelope in front of his face, his eyes widen with surprise and fury. I call for my brother and Tristan to come out of the room. Tariq looks like a little boy on Christmas Day; I can tell this will bring the peace that he has been searching for since leaving prison. "YOU SON OF A BITCH!", Chris mutters to Tariq. I respond, "You know these results will determine whether or not you live to remember this day, right?" Tariq draws his gun and points it directly to Chris's head, cocking it as I slowly open the envelope. Chris boldly utters, "I'm being murdered because I want my son? I ruined my relationship with Jasmine, I get that, but he is my son. He is not yours!"

I bark back, "You have some nerve to mention my wife's name after all you put her through! I don't know what's up with this infatuation you have with my family, but I will put us all out of misery tonight! You almost ruined my damn business, you tried to destroy my marriage, and the last straw was my blood brother! You manipulated him into robbing a bank to frame me—you sick bastard! You sought out every possible trap to take me down, yet I am here prevailing over you. I let you live four years ago, and you're still not happy."

"Bullshit! The only way to prove I'm right is to read the results."

"You know, Chris, I wanted this to be easy for you. Ty, pass me this bastard key." I pick up the chair that Chris is chained to and throw him in the back of my SUV. "Ty, you take my car, I'll take his. Follow me; don't take one wrong turn."

We arrive at a chop shop and I let my homeboy know what's going on. He responds, "Oh, you brought some extra shit for me to grind? Let me handle this lightweight, bro." This shit was like Jason's Lyric, and I feel sorry for Chris, but he has crossed me one too many times. For all I know, he could've been planning to kill my son once the test proves that he is not the father. I wipe my fingerprints off of the steering wheel and car handle. I told Tristan to Uber to the chop shop so we can make the next move. When he saw the severity of the situation, he asked me, "Are you sure about this? I mean, I can get you off, no doubt. But will your conscious be able to handle this?" I was quiet for a second, then replied, "I am as sure about this as I am that I am the father of that little boy."

Chapter 14: Antonio Part II

There's Nothing More to Say

My people at the chop shop loan me a vehicle without asking for too many details. I told them to blow up Christopher's car and leave no trace of it ever coming there. I order Tariq to go to my house and keep an eye on Chris. Christopher's fate will be served on a cold dish, and I will mercilessly prepare him for it. I gave Tariq permission to torture Chris until he grew tired; of course, he had a field day doing so. Tristan and I go to his office to discuss the logistics of how we would legally get away with murder. I am forever indebted to Tristan for risking not only his livelihood but also his freedom. He is the only brother that I know who has never seen the back of a police car, and he only visits a courtroom when he is defending a case. He is not only protecting me but setting an example for Jr. that neither Chris nor I could ever demonstrate. My family, my house, my life, and my sanity are all in shambles, but thanks to my legal team, a loyal brother, and a wife who's a rider, I know that I will claim victory. I cannot fuck this up, and I won't allow Chris to infringe on my family's happiness any longer.

I leave the office before Tristan so I can check on my brother. I confiscated Chris's cell phone and instructed Tariq to call only if Chris somehow became unconscious. As the Uber eases into my driveway, I ask God for my son to never learn about any of this until he is a grown man. Whether science declares him as my son or not, I am the only father he knows. I hope Chris has asked for forgiveness; today is his final hour. I walk in my home and see that Tariq has cleared out all of the furniture from the den, placed a tarp on the floor, and chained Chris to a chair. When Chris realizes I am at the door he bellows, "I don't care how long I endure this torture! It is worth it for MY son! You can kill me, but I will live forever because Jr. is MY son!" He jerks the chair so ferociously that he manages to break one of its legs. I look down on him and aim my gun at his head, but I decided to hit him in the mouth with it instead of shooting him. I blow the other three legs off the chair; I must admit, it is a pleasure to sabotage Chris. But as a man, I can't torture him too long. I am ready to off him and be done with the situation.

Tristan arrives with a manila envelope in his hand and urges us to wrap up the process; there is no point in lingering the plan. "Antonio, I have to speak with you privately before we leave. Tariq, start the car." Christopher interrupts Tristan by saying, "You can't kill me and get away with it!" Tariq cuts him off, "Chris, don't act like you want to be Super Dad! You've been venting about your hatred toward my brother ever since you got me out of prison!" Tristan was recording the entire ordeal on his phone. I cut my brother off, "You are a pitiful piece of shit who has manipulated anyone you possibly could so that you can destroy my life. Let's keep it real; you could give two shits about MY SON; you are here to avenge Jasmine for choosing me over you. From blackmailing my brother to sending a DNA test to my in-laws, you have been trying your damnedest to ruin my marriage. You forgot that you disclose your escape plan to my brother, huh? Didn't you know my brother is my keeper?" Chris begins to sob uncontrollably, pleading for us to talk it out. "Antonio, everything you're saying is correct, but can we please talk this out?"

"Talk! Talk about what?! Talk about how you brought the feds to my club and had them send me a cease and desist letter? Talk about how you tried to get my brother to set me up? Talk about how you tried to steal my firstborn son? Man, you can save your speech for your maker, because you'll be meeting Him sooner than you think!" Tristan passes me a shot of Tequila and tells me that his office dug a bit deeper into the situation. "Bro, I don't know what these results say, but I think you should read them before we blow this sucker's head off." I inhale, take the shot, and rip open the manila folder. I stare at the results and tears welled into my eyes. The silence was deafening; I continued to read in disbelief. It read, "Based on the DNA samples provided by each party, it is proven that Mr. Antonio Jennings is not the biological father of Antonio Jerami Jennings, Jr." The expression on my face says I need another shot. I grab the bottle and continue to read. "Based on our analysis, it is practically proven that Mr. Christopher Leon Davis is the biological father of the Antonio Jerami Jennings, Jr."

I drink the whole bottle of Tequila in one gulp. "Are you satisfied, now? My heart has been ripped from my chest right in front of you! I don't give a damn about those results; I am still raising him as a JENNINGS!" Chris started laughing; saying, "I told y'all, y'all will never see MY son again. And you thought I cared about your whore of a wife? What kind of mother doesn't know who the father of her kid is?" I picked up the gun, pointed it in his mouth and cocked it. "You say anything else about Jasmine, and I'm going to make you eat this bullet." As soon as I was about to pull the trigger, Tristan hollered for me to stop immediately. "Antonio, wait! My secretary is on speakerphone, and she has real results from the lab! Go ahead, Laura."

"Antonio, I just spoke with someone at the lab, they drove to Ohio to provide us with the correct information! We have been informed that Christopher Davis bribed one of the newer lab technicians into switching the results. You ARE the father, and the previous test results are fraudulent." I fall to my knees to praise God for answering my prayers. I scold Chris and shoot him twice in his chest. "I told you this is MY family and nobody can take that away from me!" He took his last breath with his eyes fixed on mine; my brother took the gun out of my hand. "I'll clean this up; go get yourself situated. Now we can put this behind us."

Chapter 15: Tariq

Drastic Measures

My brother has finally settled the debt of revenge that Chris had been begging for, and I was more than happy to be his accomplice. Chris has knocked on heaven's door too many times, so he finally got his request: death. After this is behind us, I am going to skip town my damn self and get a fresh start. Even though Chris was a pain in the ass, if it weren't for his schemes, I would still be in the penitentiary. The grief that Chris has caused my family is unbelievable, but it's all behind us now. This is the last dead body I am burying for the rest of my days on earth. I deserve a successful life without the criminal shenanigans, and after this is all over, I will live a successful life just like my brother. If he's able to live the good life after all the dirt he's done, I am sure I can turn my life around, too. Now, all I need to do is bury Chris without leaving a trace.

I paid the chop shop owner to rent me an unmarked white van to drive to the destination. I wore a completely black ensemble: jumpsuit, gloves, and sneakers. I burned his fingerprints off with acid, poured acid over his face, and wrapped him up in the tarp. We need to be entirely untraceable; I need to make him unidentifiable as possible. In a way, I am happy that I am the one discarding his body, it's like an apology to my brother. Even though Chris blackmailed me, I am a grown-ass man and responsible for my actions. I'm sure Antonio is completely out of the game now that there aren't any more threats to his family.

Before Jasmine came along my brother was a ruthless motherfucker. He was a trigger-happy gangster who dared anyone to cross him. But ever since he's started a family, no one could pay him to kill a fly. I admire that shit and hope that I am the same way when I start a family. Ant was the king of gang banging in our hood. I remember back in the day when some idiot robbed our mother's job during her shift. I guess he was new to the neighborhood and didn't know that if anyone were brave enough to cross our mother without saying excuse me, they were liable to see Antonio— *personally*. As soon as my mother called Antonio with a description of the robber, my brother had his goons kidnap him from his home. When he got to Antonio's basement, he was greeted with a kick in the groin and chained to a chair in front of the television. My brother played the news clip of the robbery, which happened to show my mom crawling under her register. He made the mistake of not wearing gloves, so the birthmark on his right hand incriminated him.

"You know that was my mother's store you robbed, right? You know she's afraid to go back to work now? And did you know that I have goons on every corner, guards at every mall, bakery, supermarket, bank, strip club—you name it! All I ever ask is that my community keeps my family safe, and I will keep them safe in return. I run this shit! It seems your posse neglected to send you the memo. And who the fuck robs a place with no gloves on? Well, since you don't value my mother's life, you don't value my life. And, since you didn't bother to conceal your hands, you obviously don't value those either. So, I'll do the cops a favor and teach you a lesson myself." Antonio chainsawed the man's right thumb and index finger, making it impossible to attempt to pull a trigger ever again. The agonizing cry that spewed from his soul was solid enough to remind everyone that Antonio's name still held weight. Of course, I did the dirty work and sent him on a one-way Greyhound bus to Oregon. That's how it was; we both do the dirt, but I am the one cleaning it up. Like I said, I take full responsibility in the role I played in this situation. Nonetheless, I am ready to live my life, too.

Well, so much for going down memory lane. I lit a fat ass blunt and inhaled the sweet essence of nature's goodness. The aroma was potent enough to cut the reeking smell of Chris' body. I decided to cut his body in pieces before I dump his punk ass all over Tennessee. I take a bottle of Hennessy to the head before I leave the van to dig a hole for his body. I grab a shovel and start to dig until I see a frightening abyss of darkness. Chris is about to meet the devil face to face after I throw his body into this hole. My heart was beating a mile a minute, but I maintain my composure. I go back to the van and drag his body all the way to the hole and watch it plummet 6ft down the hole. After covering his body with the dirt, I realize that I am also burying my past. I mean it, I am not about this street thuggin lifestyle anymore. I spit on his ghetto ass grave and haul ass back to Atlanta.

I left my phone at home to avoid any towers from tracking my route. The drive was a grueling six hours back to Atlanta. The owner of the chop shop was expecting my arrival at 6:00 am., and I was not a second late. I changed my clothes and tossed them into the burning firewood in the back of the shop. I chose to walk the two-hour trek home so I can meditate on my new life.

Chapter 16: Jasmine

A Fresh Start

North Carolina has been a breath of fresh air that I needed to regroup and prioritize my life. Antonio and I have never been separated for this long; in fact, we've never been separated at all! Chris has come in like a thief in the night and attempted to destroy the only thing that I live for; however, my superman of a husband took care of his ass with no hesitation. Antonio refuses to tell me all of the details because he fears that I will resent him for going back to his past lifestyle for the sake of our family. In reality, I am grateful to have a protective husband who will literally kill for his family.

I am in the process of forgiving myself for causing all of this confusion. I should have stopped messing around with Chris long before I had done so, especially since I was confident that Antonio would one day be my husband. I was trying to win Chris back from his little concubine but still wanted to entertain a tryst with Antonio. Never would I have imagined that Chris would come back into our lives to wreak havoc. As fate would have it, Antonio is the only father that Jr. will know of; thank God my past carelessness did not ruin my picture-perfect life.

Nonetheless, I can't wait to see my husband after this all over. This is the one time that I am looking forward to carpet burn, sweaty sheets, and endless rounds of passion-filled sex! The pain and frustration that I have built up inside of me can only be released into my King, and vice versa. My yoni is yearning for his masculine touch, plus my fellatio is on fire! He is going to get the reward of a lifetime for saving our family from tragedy. His warm embrace is as ensuring as the bear hugs my Dad gave me when I was a little girl. It won't be long before Antonio arrives at my parent's house, and my panties are getting wetter by the day. In the meantime, I will put on my big girl lingerie and continue to work on our North Carolina lounge location.

While on speakerphone, I expressed my concerns about establishing a new lounge in North Carolina. "Baby, the night-life here is not nearly as vibrant as it is in Atlanta. You've been gone for too long. I miss you so much; it's starting to make me sick." I feel a bit discouraged about the new venture. I am capable of making excellent business decisions, but since Antonio has been handling Chris, I feel like I am doing everything alone.

He reassures me "Jas, listen, we can shake things up a bit to distinguish it from our Atlanta location, but we still have to do it. I know I haven't been as present as you would like me to be, but trust me, I am making life better for both of us. This shit is hard on me, too, but that's why I need my Queen to hold shit down. And stop speaking blasphemy about our business, this is your dream just much as it is mine. You would be sick to your stomach if you did not bring your interior decorating dreams to life. Don't worry; everything will be back to normal and I'll be home later. The only thing I need you to do is keep our business afloat. Daddy will be home later." My King always has the most encouraging words in the darkest hours. As hubby said, it's back to business. Although I am impatiently awaiting his return, I am going to make him proud by pouring all of my energy into our new business. I schedule a meeting with the real estate manager to solidify the details of the lounge; it will be an upscale restaurant lounge that requires RSVP for each entry. Since the millennial crowd in North Carolina is not as electrifying as Atlanta's, I will have to prioritize entry to show them that it's exclusive.

The property manager, Mrs. Baker, is ecstatic to see me; she has a new receptionist who is much more hospitable than the last one. Mrs. Baker and the new receptionist greet me with mimosas and hors d'oeuvres on the bar. She sure knows how to woo her clientele! Truthfully, I was going to sign the lease regardless, but the congenial welcome sealed the deal.

"Mrs. Jennings, it is wonderful to see you again. I hope we can settle on this property for your new endeavor. I have seen the success of your Atlanta location, and I must say I am impressed. I am willing to offer you a five-year lease for your new venture, and I am also interested in being a silent investor. The demand for your chic vision is monumental, and I am confident that you and your husband will make a cash cow out of this business." I smile and update her on my business plan; I am sure Antonio will like the idea of someone else investing in our vision, especially since we have been paying for everything out of pocket.

"I am glad that you mentioned my vision for the new business. I envision it being the meet-up place for young professionals, entrepreneurs, and socialites. A dress code will be enforced, as well as a mandatory guest list. The food will be prepared in front of the guest, and the ambiance will reflect Black excellence. Smooth jazz, top-shelf liquor, a live band on certain nights, silent auctions, and networking events will define the culture of the lounge. It will be the designated venue for celebrity nightlife and a place where executives convene to close million-dollar deals. We're going to call it N'fluence. The color scheme will be gold and white; the light fixture will be a gold-tinted Atlantis Suspension Light - Long; candles will grace every table and shelf; we will have five high-top tables. The tables will be accommodated with buttoned, bucket bar stools and three sets of buttoned, tufted back booths with a padded base. All furniture will have a black matte base with gold chrome." As I was walking around her office explaining my dream, I could see that she was in awe of my detailed illustration of N'fluence.

"I have heard enough, Mrs. Jennings! I am ready to sip saké and eat sushi in my new Manolos. I have already drawn up the lease and outlined my offer as a prospective silent investor. I am prepared to invest $100,000 in cash, and I am only asking for 20 percent stake in the company. My offer is good until the end of the quarter, as I am excited to begin the venture. Talk it over with your husband and let me know what you two thinks of it." "Thank you, Mrs. Baker; we will have an answer well before the end of the quarter, the Queen City needs N'fluence."

I leave Mrs. Baker's office beaming with delight and a new-found spirit of relentlessness. My husband was right; I am the Queen of the Kingdom; I call the shots, and he approves them! Just as I was about to pull into the supermarket where Chris last spied on me in, I get a text from Antonio.

Antonio: "I am driving to North Carolina tonight."

Although I have been enjoying the retreat at my parent's house, I am elated by the news. I conquer my fears and walk into the supermarket and relinquish Chris' spirit away from me. I have no idea what my husband has done to him, but it could never be as worse than the pain he has bestowed to my family. Tears of joy begin to stream from my eyes and, before I could wipe away a single tear, the wind dries my face, and I am overwhelmed by a whiff of gratitude. I grab some groceries and hurry home to pack our clothes. I pull into my parent's driveway and can smell the fresh baked cookies before I even reach the kitchen. My heart smiles and, the joy expands when I see Daddy and my babies frolicking in a pile of leaves. My mother wastes no time putting me to work. "Jasmine, check on those biscuits in the oven, please. And put on some hot chocolate when you get a chance. Thanks, doll!" I inhale the buttery goodness and sneak one before the rest of the crew smuggles them all. I am so happy that my babies get to experience the country life; the nostalgia is all that I need to remind me that I am immensely blessed.

"Jasmine! I hear you smacking on those biscuits! Who told you that you could have one, you're just like your darn father! I hope you saved some for the rest of us; miss greedy pants!" Oh, yes, I am HOME!

"Mommy, I just love it here! Not only at home but in North Carolina in general. I never wanted to move to Atlanta, I was too busy following Chris, and his dreams led us there. Besides my business and husband, I can leave Atlanta for good. We can always hire managers to operate the lounge. If we move back here, we can all start over anew." "I hear you, baby girl, I didn't want you moving while you were in college, but you were so headstrong about it, just like my husband. We both could see through Chris, but no one can tell a girl anything when she's in love." She motions for me to pass her a knife to chop up some carrots. "You're right, but a girl can get used to Sunday dinner on a Tuesday afternoon!" Before we could go back to our conversation, my dad and kids bomb-rushed the biscuits and hot chocolate we prepared for them. My babies really keep Daddy young and in shape; I can barely tell he has arthritis. He kisses me on the forehead, confirming that I am still his baby girl. "Look, Jas, your mom and I have been thinking, and maybe you and Antonio should consider moving back home." "Here? As in with you and Mom?" My parents looked at each other and laughed hysterically. "How do you young people say it? 'You tried it!'" He gives me a list of houses that are on the market for sale. It's almost like they were reading my mind; I'm going to talk it over with Antonio, but I am sure he will side with whatever makes me happy. Plus, we can have more date nights without worrying about paying a sitter. "You're still young; you're finally married; now all we need is more grand-babies!" He slipped that in there so quickly that I almost agreed! We all laughed at my dad's half-serious, half-humorous remarks. I quickly excuse myself from the table and retreat in the den to collect my thoughts.

The smell of the roast is mesmerizing, but I am focused on devising a plan to present to my husband. I researched the list of homes my dad provided; many were ranch-style 3-5-bedroom homes with a lush yard. We could even have a stable of horses in our backyard if we wanted, the sky is really the limit with this immense amount of real estate. One listing read, "Spacious, valley-green ranch-style home nestled in a private cul-de-sac in the heart of Queen City. The suburban home is complete with stainless steel appliances, a dual flush toilet, mobile island, high ceilings, and a living room of a six-light Petal Semi-Flush vintage ceiling lights. The three-story home is ideal for a growing family of little ones and has rooms that easily convert to office space. The spacious master suite has two walk-in closets, and a jacuzzi-style bathtub accompanied by a contemporary chrome shower system. The master suite also houses an electric fireplace; the living room has an inviting wood-burning masonry fireplace and an outside view of the newly installed pond. The tankless water heater operates the laundry room and dishwasher. The charter schools in the neighborhood have excellent reviews, small class sizes, and a diverse student body. It is central to a galore of upscale department stores and outlets; the restaurants feature a cultural cuisine that also abounds the area. Say hello to your new home!" I emailed the realtor of the property and was happy to learn that she was in the same network as Mrs. Baker. This is all too good to be true; just as I was about to set up an appointment, Antonio texts me. I inform her that she can expect to hear from me within two business days.

Antonio: "I promised to take care of everything, and I did. We have nothing to worry about now; it's all behind us. Baby, I want us to have a fresh start; I think we should move back to North Carolina for good."

WOW! It's like this man has tapped inside my soul and can read my thoughts. We have that telepathic love!

Me: "It doesn't matter where I am bae, as long as I'm with you and our babies."

I recline further back into the couch and am blissfully paralyzed. My mother brings me back to reality by informing me that dinner is ready; she even made my plate! While we were fellowshipping and fantasizing about the possibilities of relocating to North Carolina, I receive a call from the realtor, Keisha Evans. "Good evening, Mrs. Jennings! I wanted to let you know that people are bidding on the home by the minute; I suggest you come to view it within the next thirty minutes." I wrap up my dinner and head straight to the property. I sent Ant the link, and he approved it immediately. Little did I know my parents and babies were trailing behind me. Keisha met us with a warm welcome and more hot chocolate, which my babies loved. Mom and dad are already planning family dinners in the dining room; we FaceTime Antonio and he can hardly stop cheesing, assuring me, "Baby, that's the one! Mrs. Evans, we will top the highest bidder—in cash!" Keisha is all smiles and exclaims, "My assistant will send the contract to your email now; all that's left to do is sign in and bring it to my office by noon tomorrow." My whole family squeals with joy, and in unison, we retort, "THANK YOU!"

Chapter 17: Tariq

It All Played Out

People who think revenge is sweet must have never tasted the savory victory of vindication. If revenge is a dish best served cold, then vindication is the arctic kitchen. Even though Chris lured me into his devilish game plan to destroy my family by offering me conditional freedom, I have to man up and take accountability for my role in it as well. I fucked up and could only see the short-term gain. I spent what felt like an eternity in the penitentiary and nearly every minute was dedicated to thinking of ways to avenge my brother. It had been years sent he had visited me, much less put money on my books. When Chris approached me with the opportunity to end my sentence on such short notice, agreed to represent me, and devised a plan to make my brother's life a living hell, I thought God had finally answered my prayers. I could not have been more wrong; Chris had used me as a pawn, and I was too vulnerable to dig deeper into the plan. I must say, Chris, conjured up a master plan, and had it not been for my loyalty to my brother, it would have worked. Thankfully, my conscience got the best of me, and I regained my integrity. I refuse to be the son of Judas and sell out the only person who has ever had my best interest at heart. No amount of freedom or money can tempt me to murder my brother.

It has only been five days since we buried Chris, and the world already seems to be less evil. His spirit was beneath contempt, and there was no room for that depth of hatred in our lives. Despite the mayhem that led up to this tragedy, I can honestly say that I am proud of Antonio and admire his commitment to his family. On the real, I can't wait until it's my turn to build a solid family. I need a Queen who won't put up with my bullshit, is a straight freak in the bed, is ready to carry my seed, and loves me for who I am. I won't find her in the strip club, so maybe I'll finally go to church one of these Sundays. But, for now, I'm going to kick it with my sandbox homie. As soon as I pull up to our old stomping grounds in the West End, the first sound I hear blazing from the speakers is "Welcome to Atlanta!" We've done so much dirt on Ralph D. Abernathy Boulevard that Atlanta should give us a key to the city! Now that I think about it, I lost my virginity in my first love's house on this same street. Her name was Kerri. Kerri was the only woman who could get me to stay in the house while my boys were throwing away their rent money at Magic City strip club. Her sex was so good that I'm surprised we don't have fifty-million babies! But that was then, and this is now; I want the woman I marry to give me those same vibes. Before I could finish my daydream, my homie says he has someone for me to meet.

"Bro, trust me; she's a dime piece." As soon as I walk in the door, I see Kerri. I'm sure I was looking like a kid in a candy store, hell, no piece of candy is as sweet as her.

"Damn, did you forget how to speak while you were locked away?" Her smart mouth always broke the ice in any tense situation. I can't help but grin and wrap my arms around her. I haven't seen her in at least a decade, but I feel as though we have not skipped a beat; I forgot my homie was watching us the whole time.

"This is not the Holiday Inn! Go get a room, lovebirds!" We walked to my car, and I lifted her onto my car's hood. I started to kiss her, but she placed her finger on my lips and told me she had something she needed to get off of her chest.

"I apologize for not visiting you while you were locked up. But I didn't know if you were going to ever come home, and I had so much hope in our relationship that I did not want to be disappointed."

This is a dream come true. Kerri is the one person who kept it real with me and gave me the tough love I needed. "No need to apologize, sweetie. I don't blame you; I still remember the words of encouragement you gave me the last time you came to the pen. You were rocking the hell out of a Jamaican-flag sundress. The bright colors made me forget about the gloominess inside of the jail cell. Your hair was cut into a layered bob and barely covered your beautiful, hazel eyes. Your fingernails and toenails were all painted Easter yellow. The way you made me feel was unforgettable. I am so happy that you even considered meeting with me again; I thought you were done with me for good. The last thing you told me was, 'Get a good look now, baby because I won't see you again until you have your shit together.'"

She was in awe of what I had just confessed to her, she tried to speak but, all she could do was cry. I embraced her and coddled her in my chest. Kerri really helped me to take life more seriously. She started to laugh and said, "I'm glad you finally got your shit together because I can't see myself with anyone else besides you." She smiles and hugs me tighter. I assure her that I am done with the street life, the partying, the fast life, everything. I am ready to start a real family and be fully committed. No more fuck-ups, I promise. I wipe her tears away and lift her head from my chest. I get on one knee in the middle of the parking lot and tell her I will have a diamond ring tomorrow if she says yes to marrying me. She covers her face with her hands and exclaims, "YES! Yes, I will marry you! I can't wait to be Mrs. Kerri Jennings!" I lift her up to the sky and stare into her wondrous eyes. Then, out of nowhere, I hear clapping. My homie called her family over to see me, and they had all gathered around us. I am overwhelmed with joy and rush to call my brother. He's become my best friend these days, and I am forever grateful. Kerri and I drive to the park near the lounge to meet Antonio. He walks up to my car, and before I could say anything, Kerri screams, "Your brother and I are getting married!"

"Are you serious, bro? Congratulations! You both deserve it." I step out of the car so Antonio and I can speak in private.

"This has been a hell of a month, huh?" Antonio let out a loud sigh of relief and I could see that a giant boulder had been lifted from his shoulders. I laughed and pulled out a blunt for us to smoke. "It sure has. But all of that is behind us now. I can't wait to double date and do corny shit with you and Jasmine. You have a lot to teach me, big bro! And for the record, I apologize for all the fucked-up shit I've done in the past. You've always been an amazing brother to me." "Bro, let's leave the past where it belongs. By now we're even." We dap up and take a few more puffs of the blunt. Kerri started to get anxious, so she honked the horn.

"May I have my fiancé back, please!" We laugh, and he gives me a manila envelope. I opened it, and it contained all of the legal documents for the lounge as well as $12,000 in cash. Each document had my name on it. "Bro, I have signed the lounger over to you. If anyone deserves it and will run it successfully, it's you."

My eyes begin to gloss; I am so grateful for my brother.

"That's not all, groom." He gives me a key that is secured on a keyring that is shaped like a house. "I also bought you a condo in Midtown Atlanta. I'm sure your new bride will enjoy it. My family is permanently relocating to North Carolina, and we won't have time to operate two large-scale businesses." I was so ecstatic that all I could do was hug him. "I appreciate you, brother."

"That's what brothers are for. You gotta bring Kerri to visit in North Carolina; Jasmine will love her." Antonio and I dap up one last time, and I share the good fortune with my fiancé. For every loss I've ever taken, this win was more than worth the wait.

Chapter 18: Antonio

Tie Up Loose Ends

Boyz II Men could not have sung it any better, "Although we've come

To the end of the road, Still I can't let go, it's unnatural, You belong to me, I belong to you." The life that Jasmine and I have built-in Atlanta will be difficult to let go, but I would rather leave the horrible memories here. If there is one thing I know for sure, it is that Jasmine and I belong together for all of eternity. The house, business, cars, clothes, and jewelry are all earthly possessions that God can take away at any time. But the love between Jasmine and I will not only stand the test of time, but it will prove that through the toughest trials our spirits will not be broken. Because of our strength, our children now have an example of what true love looks like. Since my parents were not married, I did not think it was possible to sustain a healthy, loving marriage and family.

Nonetheless, thanks to the support of Jasmine's parents, we can give our children the life that I always dreamt of living. I can't stand to be away from them any longer, so, I am loading the U-Haul and leaving the past where it leaves Atlanta belongs. Before I haul ass, there is an important business that must be handled peacefully. These days I work smarter not harder and prepare for the unknown. First thing's first is to establish a wealth plan and legacy for my wife and children. My son and daughter have a hefty college fund, and I am leaving a secret spousal account for Jasmine. Her parents will be the only ones who are aware of the spousal account, I don't want my baby splurging at Home Goods during a round of retail therapy. Now, all I have to do is close out all of our accounts in Atlanta, and we are free to enjoy a new life, debt-free.

The housekeeper/Nanny, Maria, is the only person who I trust with my children, so, it's only right to bless her before we permanently leave Atlanta. We pay her $1,500 per week, which is unheard of in Atlanta. But trust me, she is well worth it. Our children adore her; she helps with homework, chores, and even teaches them Spanish. Maria has become a part of the Jennings family and starting a new life without her will be difficult for the whole family. I am going to make sure that she doesn't have to worry about where her next meal will come from or where she will lay her head for at least six months. Maria maintains the upkeep of the garden, ensures that the whole house is dust-free each day, and can throw down in the kitchen almost as great as my Grandma! She may be Mexican, but there are Black genes somewhere in her family history.

"Hola, Maria! I have some good news and some bad news to share with you." She pauses from cleaning the living room and looks at me with misty eyes.

"Como Estas, ¿Señor Jennings?", she asks so graciously.

"The bad news is that I need you to pack our entire house into boxes, we're moving to North Carolina for good the U-haul just pulled up. Don't worry; I've hired help for you."

"Sí, Señor Jennings. I will miss los niños y tu bella esposa!"

My Spanish has definitely improved since Maria's been with us, she says that she will miss my children and beautiful wife. If she did not have a family, then I would ask her to join us in North Carolina.

"¡Maria, you never asked about the good news!"

"¿Que?"

I handed her an envelope with her first and last name on it; enclosed is the deed to our house with her name listed as the new owner paid in full. I also gave her $10,000 for vacation expenses. The utilities are paid in full for a year, and she is only required to pay the yearly taxes for the property. She trembles, pants and sobs uncontrollably.

"Maria! You don't want to soak the deed to *your* new house with those tears! I hope these are tears of joy. We will miss you and always remember your sweet spirit and authentic Mexican food. But it's time for us to move on; there is no place for us to live happily in Atlanta anymore."

"¡Gracias, Señor Jennings! How can I ever repay you?"

"Our pleasure; we owe you so much more."

Once she was able to pull herself together, she began packing our rooms very neatly. While she was doing that, I hired a construction company to redesign the 'crime scene room' so that there would be no trace of any foul play. The last person who I owe a gift is Tristan. Without him, all of our asses would be sitting in jail right now. Since he is the next Johnnie Cochran, I purchase the building for his new office space in the heart of Downtown Atlanta. He'll only have to pay property taxes each year. It will be the flagship for his youth attorney camp that he has envisioned! I love my family more than life itself, so they are my priority. Now that my brother and I have repaired our brotherhood, I am excited to be his best man! Everything seems to be falling into place perfectly; I text Jasmine to let her know that Big Daddy's on his way home, so I hope she's ready. We haven't had sex in weeks, so I know my sanctuary is tight, wet and waiting for me to give it the TLC it deserves. She replies with the cat emoji and a heart, then sends a voice message saying, "I love you, baby." The long drive to my new home gives me time to reflect on how ludicrous life has been in the past few months. First, Chris hires my brother to shatter my life into pieces. Now, Chris is dead, and Tariq is on his way to marrying the love of his life.

I can't forget about Jasmine's new lounge, which will be a successful money magnet. These are the best days of my life! After a while, I realize that a black SUV is trailing behind me, so I shift to my left lane. The SUV is following my every move. I FaceTime Jasmine so she can see that someone is following me. The all black-tinted SUV seems to have a mission to solve that involves me, but then I think that it may be my mind playing tricks on me. She begins to panic, so I told her I'd call her back after the SUV stopped stalking me.

"I love you, Jasmine, with all of my heart. You hear me?!" She tries to hide the tears, but I can see them streaming and then the video drop. I try to divert my route, but the SUV doesn't miss a beat. I finally weave my way into a neighborhood and can lose them. As soon as I was exiting the neighborhood to return to the highway, the SUV cuts in front of me, making it impossible to escape. I quickly shove my briefcase under the passenger's seat. I look up from the seat and see Chris's brother Curtis pointing a gun through the window. For once in my life, I am nervous about grabbing my gun.
"Remember me, motherfucker! I am my brother's keeper!"

Chapter 19: Jasmine

This Is How It All Ends

It is becoming harder and harder for me to fake the funk to our children. They ask non-stop questions about their daddy, they have been fighting more than usual, and Jr. is starting to have a temper. My father tries to discipline, but he needs Antonio's strong voice to intimidate Jr. Our baby girl told me that she misses her daddy's forehead kisses and bedtime stories. I have been a little lonely, too. Since that frantic call from him didn't put my frustrations at ease.

He FaceTime's me as soon as I was about to take a nap. Before I can say anything, he frantically starts rambling about loving me and the children more than life itself. Beads of sweat are cascading down his face, and I begin to hyperventilate into an anxiety attack. He mumbles that a black SUV is following his every move; he thinks that someone has a hit out on him. He promises to call me back as soon as he loses track of the stalker. My stomach has an unsettling feeling; I try to remain calm under pressure, but I can't. I dial Tristan's work-line, but his receptionist tells me that he's in court. She asks to take my message, but all I can do is bawl and wail loudly.

"They're trying to hurt my husband! I can't take this shit! Please tell Tristan it is a family emergency."

"Yes, Mrs. Jennings. He will call you as soon as the court goes into recess."

I hang up with her to call Tariq. He can sense the weariness in my voice when I speak.

"Jasmine, what's wrong! Calm down, who hurt you? Are the children OK?"

I squeal, "SOMETHING IS WRONG! Someone is after my Antonio! I saw a black SUV chasing him, and—"

I gasp for air and try to listen to Tariq. I blurt out "OH MY GOD! WHY WON'T THIS SHIT END! Do something Tariq, please, go save him." My body goes numb.

"What! Track his phone, Jasmine!"

"Tariq, I don't know what to do; Tristan is in court. I am about to call the police."

"HELL NO! DON'T CALL THE POLICE! Call Tristan again. Send me his location, sis." I'm on the way.

Somehow, I manage to go into my settings and add Tariq to our shared navigation tracker. Technology is amazing.

Tristan finally returns my call, and I tell him that something suspicious is happening with Antonio. I don't know what to do.

He is dead silent, and I can tell that he knows something.

"Jasmine, I have something to tell you. Someone dropped a note in my office this morning. I finally sat down to read it, and I was stoic. I need you to sit down Jasmine before I read this, but it is better coming from me then someone else. It reads:

"My brother, Chris, knew he wasn't the father of Jr. He wanted to make Antonio pay and make Jasmine suffer since she sabotaged his life. Antonio stole my brother's life away from him like a thief in the night. What began as a lofty idea

spawn into an unimaginable nightmare. One that Chris was never able to leave in the night. He made his mind up to destroy Antonio's life, and in the process, he lost his. I haven't heard from my brother in a week. He warned me that Antonio and his brother were going to avenge him, but I'm not sure if he knew it meant death. I'm sorry that Jasmine has to endure the pain, but it is the same pain that I know too well. Chris may not have meant anything to you all, but he was everything to me. You got your beloved son, why did you have to kill him? You understand I am coming for Antonio, right? I will not stop until he reaches his final rest. I understand Tariq will come looking for me, so may the best man win."

    I don't have any more tears to cry, my voice is hoarse, and I lay in a pool of sweat. My mind immediately flashes back to the beginning of my relationship with Chris; then I see the chaos between Claire and Antonio. A montage of my entire life from the day I set foot in Atlanta is playing in my mind like a horror movie. How can one unintentional relationship cause a chain of unforeseen casualties? I lost everything during attempting to keep my family together. First, my husband, to whom I vowed to spend my life. The father of my kids is dead. Is this real?! Time is at a standstill; tears are falling, but I can't feel any emotions.

    I can't believe that this tragedy is happening on the first night in our new home. It was not supposed to happen this way; Antonio and I were supposed to christen every room with our sweet love. Jr. and Jada were supposed to make memories in their new home; I was supposed to bake the cookies while their father built a custom treehouse. My dream was finally coming true; now the grim reaper is attempting to steal it away from me again! I will trade the grandeur house, thriving business, and any other assets that Antonio and I have if it means that I can see him one last time.

Tariq arrives at my house at the same time as the police, and he assures me that he will be the father figure that my children need. As much as I appreciate his support, I WANT MY HUSBAND BACK! I don't have the strength to reply, so I nodded my head in agreeance as my face and eyes suffer the heat of my tears. The police got out the car with a solemn disposition. They sadly inform us of what they saw at the scene.

"Mrs. Jennings, we found your husband's briefcase under the passenger's seat; his body was buried in a ditch in Georgia. We searched it thoroughly, which is how we learned your new address. I commend your husband for having all his ducks in a row; the money and guns are both legally registered. The documents in the briefcase rightfully belong to you, especially since your name is labeled as the executor of the will. We arrived at the scene only a few hours after the culprit buried Antonio and escaped. We are continuing the investigation on this case, so please bear with us as we find new evidence. We send our condolences to your family during this difficult time."

I helplessly fall into Tariq's arms and cry until the tears cease to flow. Nothing can console me. At this point, my life is over.

Outro: Tariq Wedding

June 30th

Life has a divine way of revealing God's plan for our lives, even when we are lost in the sauce! Marrying my future wife, Kerri, is the greatest gift that I have ever received. She not only loves me unconditionally, but she is carrying my first child, Antonio Tariq Jennings. If it were not for the sacrifices that Antonio made, none of this would be possible. A year after my brother was murdered Kerri found out she was pregnant. I knew that God had blessed us with a son, not to replace Antonio, but to continue the Jennings legacy. Jr and Jasmine will have a playdate. The bond that Kerri and Jasmine share is beautiful, and I pray that little Antonio and I will have the same relationship. Kerri is a grievance counselor, so she has been counseling Jasmine every day, going on girls' trips, and spending quality time. I bet my future son is in heaven rejoicing with his uncle as we speak!

My brother is our guardian angel, and as bad as I would have liked to keep the saga of revenge going, I don't think Antonio would approve. I can't lie though; the thoughts of revenge sometimes consume my brain. But I ignore the temptation because I already know the outcome. My nephew, niece, and new son needs a strong man in their lives, not in the cemetery or prison. I will be the man that Antonio taught me to be and make sure that our children remember his name.

Even though I am walking down the aisle to meet the love of my life, I still can't believe that my brother won't be my best man. We chose to get married in the same venue as Jasmine and Antonio in Myrtle Beach. I wasn't able to attend their wedding, but Antonio's spirit was very present at mine! Antonio Jr. was the ring bearer; his baby girl, Jada, was the flower girl. Jasmine gifted my lovely bride with a wedding dress, a makeover, and served as her maid of honor. The waves from the beach gracefully blessed us with a fresh breeze. The divine scent of the beach offers a sweet aroma that I can taste. The blessings continue to overflow, and I am forever grateful.

I can't even explain in words how happy I am to marry the woman of my dreams, finally. While getting dressed upstairs, I overhear my future brother-in-law, Rashad, spitting game to Jasmine. If he weren't my fiancé's blood brother, I would have whipped his ass! But to be honest, I know he is a good man; Jasmine doesn't deserve to be a single mother. He sounds so corny and slick at the same time. I hear him saying, "I am an active father figure for my niece and nephew. I take little man to his basketball games and my niece in ballet. I am not a father yet, but I know I would make a great one!" Jasmine smirks a little bit before she responds, "Well, we're all family now, so, I am sure I will have a chance to meet them."

He reminds her that they aren't *really* family. "We aren't blood; we're in-laws. Don't be a stranger, beautiful lady."

Meeting my wife at the altar was the most intense moment of my life. I was like a little boy in grade-school; butterflies were fluttering nonstop, my eyes watered once I unveiled her face. Our sweet, passionate kiss made me forget about any other woman I had ever been with. The whole audience cheered us on, and soon the butterflies flew away. We released white doves for my brother, and I swear I saw the heavens open. A gleaming light shone on us all, and we have God and

Antonio to thank for it. After the wedding, we threw a big ass party! Everyone was dancing, enjoying good cocktails, and watching the men scurry away from the wedding garter while the women bombard Kerri for the bouquet. I will cherish this moment until the end of time. Once the reception was nearing an end, my wife, Jasmine, Rashad, and I stepped out on the patio to catch a breeze. The children are playing in the shallow beach, and Kerri massages her belly and smile. This is truly a dream come true! The only part that is missing is Antonio, but we can all feel him in our spirits. We each pour libations for Antonio and took a moment of silence to reflect. I lean in to kiss my bride on the cheek and admire her ring. That was the best $12,000 I have ever spent—cash-money!

"Awwww! Look at the lovebirds!" Jasmine and Rashad sing in unison. They look at each other and blush; Kerri and I can feel the chemistry that is brewing between both of them. Rashad made a toast to new, everlasting love. He says some mushy-gushy things about my wife and me, then gazes at Jasmine.

"I know the last year has been pure hell for you. If you let me, I want to show you that there's still hope in true love. I want to get to know your kids more and be the father that some coward stole from them. The smiles on their faces bring me such joy, a joy that I never want to leave my life. I would love for us to be together—as friends first, and hopefully more than friends in the future. I know it will take time, but I am here for you. Are you willing to give me that chance?"

He extended his hand toward Jasmine, and she paused to look at us before nodding her head yes with tears flowing from her eyes.

"Yes, Rashad, I am ready to take this risk with you. I couldn't think of a better person to journey this new life with." We all tapped our glasses to cheer a toast of happy beginnings.

Everything is going to be okay.

The End.

To be continued in the threequel, Toxic III:

Special Acknowledgements

Thank you for reading my books and investing in my career as an author! I would like to thank my best friend, Jasi, and my favorite cousin, Jessica, for supporting me throughout the entire writing process. Shout out to my cousin, Tiffany, for introducing me to my editor, Kalina https://www.linkedin.com/in/kalina-harrison-1a122579! Shout out to my book designer, Angel Bearfield https://www.facebook.com/dynastys.coverme! I must acknowledge my family and friends, who have showered me with love and support on my journey as an author, especially Gabe & Amariya. You can find me on FB Twitter and IG: Queen Ink Publishing. http://Www.QueenInkPublishing.com.

Dedicated to my favorite cousin, Gary Jenkins; September 8, 1970 - May 12, 2019

Dedicated to my special friend, Ashley "A-Town" Anderson; May 5, 1989 - May 5, 2009

Please stay tuned for future titles and movies! All reviews are welcome! On Amazon Website and Facebook page.

CPSIA information can be obtained
at www.ICGtesting.com
Printed in the USA
LVHW082028250919
632263LV00020B/346/P

9 781082 066887